Summer in Vermont

North Shore Retirement Community

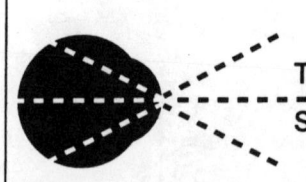

This Large Print Book carries the
Seal of Approval of N.A.V.H.

Summer in Vermont

Rebecca Marsh

Thorndike Press • Thorndike, Maine

© Copyright, 1955, by Arcadia House

All rights reserved.

Published in 1994 by arrangement with Donald MacCampbell, Inc.

Thorndike Large Print ® Candlelight Series.

The tree indicium is a trademark of Thorndike Press.

The text of this Large Print edition is unabridged.
Other aspects of the book may vary from the original edition.

Set in 16 pt. News Plantin by Melissa Harvey.

Printed in the United States on acid-free, high opacity paper. ∞

Library of Congress Cataloging in Publication Data

Marsh, Rebecca, 1916–
    Summer in Vermont / by Rebecca Marsh.
       p.   cm.
    ISBN 0-7862-0048-0 (alk. paper : lg. print)
    1. Man-woman relationships — Vermont — Fiction. 2. Large type books. I. Title.
[PS3527.E598S86 1994]
813'.54—dc20   93-27184

Summer in Vermont

CHAPTER 1

Halfway up the block the big fellow with the shock of golden hair stopped under a maple tree to rest. He had the usual audience of dogs and youngsters, but of that fact he seemed unaware. He drew a black leather pouch from his jacket pocket and from that pouch he extracted first a pipe and then a generous wad of tobacco. When the smoke had been properly prepared he snapped a lighter into flame and sucked the flame down into the pipe bowl. Almost at once twin streamers of smoke darted from his nose, and one of the youngsters giggled and confided: "Pa does that, too." The youngsters and their dogs then inched closer to the stranger. They'd be pals if he wanted pals, but the decision was clearly up to him.

The big man glanced about at the houses and yards of James Monroe Street. At that hour there was little to see, because all the men were still at work and most of the women were busy indoors with their mid-afternoon chores or small pleasures. Yet there was interest in the scene spread before him, a clean, golden spring charm he seemed to perceive in an instant and which appeared to satisfy him totally. He stood there quietly for perhaps five minutes, just smoking his pipe, gazing from house to house as if to impress their distinctions upon his memory. "What does he see?" Mrs. Wolfe asked curiously. "What on earth does he see?" Laura Staley didn't know. She imagined he was seeing a street he'd liked to live in, but of course she couldn't be sure. Anyway, she thought, it was unimportant. The important thing was to get the Staley yard properly raked and the flower beds properly spaded. Those things accomplished, she'd have the weekend free and clear. She could help Brad tidy up his barn. It was doubtful that Brad could rent his barn, but if he wanted to try to, who was she to discourage him?

"He's a salesman," Mrs. Wolfe said firmly. "Salesmen behave that way, have you ever noticed?"

"He's too relaxed, Mrs. Wolfe. He's too well-dressed, for that matter. A tweed suit of that quality and fit costs around two hundred dollars. How do I know? I've been doing some research for Brad."

"Well, what do you guess?"

Laura studied the stranger again. He was in a half-crouch now, and was scratching the floppy ears of Joady McWhinn's cocker spaniel. The dog was squealing happily and Joady was bragging about his dog and the stranger was listening attentively to both, an easy, friendly smile on his good-looking face. A doctor? A teacher? It was difficult to guess.

"He's a politician," Laura teased. "He handles the small fry almost as expertly as you do."

Mrs. Wolfe chuckled softly. "Uh-uh. A politician would just happen to have a few odd candy bars in his pocket. You get good value from a candy bar. You delight a kid, you delight the kid's family, and the expense is deductible as a business expense. I still say he's a salesman."

"Well, it doesn't matter, does it?"

An English sparrow whizzed in, a plump one. Its destination was the white, classic-style birdbath standing a dozen feet or so from the glassed-in corner of the porch. But the bird didn't fly directly to the birdbath. First it landed on the porch roof, where it "chipped" several times in the mellow May sunshine. Next it flew to another coign of vantage on the arching branch of the lilac bush. Its beady eyes flicked about quickly in all directions, and it was a silent bird now as it appraised the women over near the apple tree.

"Now there," Mrs. Wolfe announced, "is

a creature who *could* be a politician. Notice he doesn't take good will for granted? I myself never do. I find that whenever I do I'm invariably disappointed."

"You wouldn't care to help me, would you?"

It scored!

Mrs. Wolfe winced and groaned, as with pain.

Laura chuckled. "Not to be personal, of course, but some honest work would do you good."

"My dignity, dear, my dignity!"

Now the stranger's presence on the street was forgotten. Mayor Rachel Wolfe of Saunder's Bluff, Vermont, returned to the chair under the apple tree. She crossed her thick legs awkwardly and tugged the hem of her brown wool skirt down over her knees. "Furthermore," she said crisply, "you should hire a gardener. If the Staleys can't afford one, who can? I know several gardeners who need work."

"We're misers, you see."

"And as I've already said, this is a business call. I've received a complaint about that new sign on the hotel. In fact, I've received several complaints. It's considered a menace. It's also argued that the sign violates Ordinance 342, and in the opinion of our district attorney it really does."

"Talk to my father, Mayor Wolfe. It was his idea."

"I did try to do that."

"Oh?"

Now the English sparrow took the risk. It darted to the birdbath. It took a sip of the sparkling water. Then into the water it hopped to bathe while the day was still warm. It splashed, it fluttered its wings, it ducked its head. In the country quiet all this could be heard as well as seen, and to Laura's ears the sounds were pleasant. She must remember to tell Brad, she thought, that life in a small town was good because people of small towns were so close to all life.

"Your father, Laura, invited me to remember that I'm Mayor because of him. He also invited me to remember that without his support I won't be re-elected next year."

It irritated Laura. She was being distracted from her work, which was bad enough, and she was being drawn into something ugly, which was worse. In the hope Mrs. Wolfe would take the hint, she turned and jabbed her spade into the flower bed. She thrust the spade down deeper with her foot, and with an expert twist and heave got another ten pounds or so of earth nicely turned. Carefully, she broke up the rich black clods.

Mrs. Wolfe's eyes narrowed. "Understand

this, dear. I'd prefer not to battle your father. But laws are laws. I won't be bribed into overlooking violations of our laws, nor will I be intimidated by veiled threats. I'm this way, you —"

But at that point she was interrupted. The peace and quiet of James Monroe Street was suddenly shattered. There were squeals and shouts and giggles and excited barks. The big stranger was on the move again, openly attended now by the dogs and youngsters who'd apparently found a certain relief from boredom in the process of picking up a pal. There was an incident, of course. A recent graduate from the diaper set tripped over a dog and crashed to the sidewalk under the maples. The startled dog yiped. The toddler howled. But the big stranger had the answer to all that. "Easy does it," he suggested in soothing bass tones, and he scooped the toddler up to a perch on his broad shoulder. And he strode on with a smiling composure as if he were accustomed to such burdens and such a hullabaloo all around him. He made such a grand and friendly sight that even Mayor Rachel Wolfe overcame her natural aversion for "outsiders." "Nice," she commented. "I approve young fellows who have time for kids. Such a fellow has sound instincts."

"Stop picking on Brad!"

"Was I?"

"And as for the sign, that's Dad's business. I have nothing to do with it, and I won't be involved."

"The law is the law. And I just thought you'd —"

But the bedlam, coming closer, again interrupted Mayor Wolfe. She gestured irritably, glancing wistfully at the English sparrow as it flew off to the safety and quiet of another street.

"Miz Wolfe!" howled Joady McWhinn. "Miz Wolfe, Mr. Albright wants you. There she is, Mr. Albright, the fatty."

Mayor Rachel Wolfe took the description like a politician. She struggled up from her chair, smiling all the way. "Well, will you think it over?" she asked Laura. "Will you agree to do that?"

Since it would cost her nothing, Laura nodded. "As you wish. But I promise nothing, naturally."

"Naturally." With majestic aplomb Mayor Wolfe nodded and turned and trudged down the brick path toward the gate. She had a friendly greeting for all, including the freckled Joady. She just "happened to have" a few of the before-mentioned candy bars in her handbag, and she distributed them in an artful fashion, with a nice display of impartiality. That the candy bars happened to land on the grubby palms of the offspring of her strongest supporters was purely coincidental, of course. She kept up a running stream of chatter while she gave the candy to the chosen, and Laura was interested to notice that the stranger was enjoying the spectacle quite as much as she was. A business-man, she decided, who was involved in public relations just as the Mayor was. Yet he could have been an actor, for that matter. His face, warmly and solidly handsome, certainly wouldn't have been out of place on a motion picture or television screen. How many girls did he have chasing after him? A zillion? Or was he already married? He was certainly well enough groomed to be married — or was she being silly?

Mayor Wolfe now turned to him, holding out her hand cordially. "Delighted to meet you, Mr. Albright. I must state you're much younger than I thought you'd be. Welcome to Saunder's Bluff. Have you a room?"

"I'm nicely settled, Mayor Wolfe. I've been enjoying your town. It's typically New England, isn't it?"

"Yes, Mr. Albright, that young lady you're gawking at chances to be real. Miss Laura Staley, may I present Mr. Ken Albright?"

Shooting was too good for her, Laura decided, but she smiled sweetly at the two. "How do you do, Mr. Albright."

"How do you do, Miss Staley?"

The atmosphere now grew sparky. "Young man," Mrs. Wolfe announced, "I have no intention of changing my mind. I wrote you to that effect. However, since you've made this long trip, I will give you an official hearing. Shall we go to my office?"

"That would be very kind of you, Mayor Wolfe."

The procession, with Mrs. Wolfe a part of it now, moved on once more in the general direction of Franklin D. Roosevelt Avenue. Significantly, it was the Mayor who did all the talking, and Laura rather pitied the good-looking fellow, because when the Mayor's tongue was going full gallop nothing could bring it up short. She chuckled and stood watching them all until they were out of sight. Then, sobering, she went back into the cool, quiet house. She listened, heard the typewriter clacking in her father's study, and hurried to the last left-hand door down the hall. She didn't bother to knock. She made herself comfortable in the green leather chair near the desk and stared intently at the semi-bald gray-fringed head until her father swung around from the typewriter testily. She then glanced beyond him at the oil portrait of her mother on the rear wall. She resembled her mother, she told herself. She had that same short, curly, glossy black hair. She had those same wide-spaced, lustrous gray eyes. Probably her smile wasn't so wise but possibly it was as merry. In any event, since he'd loved her mother deeply, he must surely love her, and what risk was there, really, in offending him? None, she decided; and thus encouraged, she was deliberately tough.

"Nasty, Pop. Just plain old-fashioned nasty."

He glared.

Laura glared back.

"Isn't it possible, Laura, that you haven't been told the full story?"

"I'll concede the possibility, of course."

He muttered sarcastically: "Your sense of fair play touches me. Now suppose we discuss this as if we were two intelligent human beings. In the first place, that sign cost a thousand dollars. It cost two hundred dollars more to get it hung where it is. It would cost two hundred dollars to remove it, and since it isn't usable elsewhere, my total loss would come to fourteen hundred dollars. I dislike wasting money."

"If it's a violation it's a violation. And you ought to be ashamed! Pop, that sort of thing went out with bustles. I mean, you can't expect to run this town as though you own it. You don't. It's as simple as that."

He pursed his lips. He always did so under the stress of a strong emotion, and Laura mentally braced herself for a tirade on the subject of minding one's own business. Her father limited himself, however, to a sniff. This was followed by a gesture of his hand that could have meant anything, and then he walked across the small, paneled, comfortably furnished study to the windows outlooking the rear yard. He slipped his hands into the back pockets of his pin-striped black trousers. He craned somewhat to get a better glimpse of the flower bed against the house. "You know," he said, "this work could be done by a hired man. I've had several requests for work recently. It seems that one of the factories is retooling, or something, and that a number of people have been temporarily laid off."

"You won't listen to me, in other words?"

He turned, quirking a shaggy eyebrow. He said bluntly: "You're unqualified to speak, Laura. This is a business matter. You won't become involved in the business in any capacity. You therefore have no official standing; you are unqualified to speak. Isn't it as simple and logical as all that?"

Laura drew a deep breath. "You're really trying to change the subject, Pop."

"No." He was gruff now, but unbending. "You can't refuse to have anything to do with the business one minute, and then seek to interfere the next minute. If you expect to be heard you must earn the right to be heard. You must carry responsibility. For example, do I interfere with any of your decisions affecting this house? I don't, because you run the house, not I."

"And now we come to Brad. I'm a child, I'm too naïve for my own good, I'm a gay and reckless child riding for a fall. How far we've strayed from the subject!"

"I would listen to you, of course, if you agreed to enter the business. In all probability I'd favorably consider your suggestion to have the sign taken down. That's all I intend to say. Until then, since I carry the burden of the whole business on my shoulders, I expect to be permitted to run my affairs as I think they should be run."

Laura jumped up, furious. "If you'd help Brad, if you'd take him into the business, you wouldn't have such a burden."

Her father returned to his desk. He arranged himself comfortably in his swivel-chair.

"But what do you do, Dad? You oppose Brad, you try to break us up. And what happens when Brad and I are married? What sort of family relations will we have then?"

"I naturally hope you won't be that stupid."

"It isn't stupid. It's love. It's why you married Mom."

"Oh, has he agreed to marry you? I was under the impression he was still unsatisfied with his income, still unsure he could support you as you deserve to be supported."

It hurt, as it had been designed to. Laura went pale. Her gray eyes dilated. She took a step toward his desk, her lips working, her dimpled chin trembling. But somehow she managed to cling to the last remnants of her temper. "You're unfair," she managed to say huskily. "One instant you condemn Brad because he's marrying me for security. The next instant you condemn him because he won't marry me until he's earning an adequate income. Do you know what, Dad?"

"Well?"

"I think that if Mom were alive she'd say for shame, too."

He called out then, but she continued hotly to the door. Little tears blurred her eyes. The staircase swam in her vision, the old papered hall, the table supporting the old-fashioned telephone near the living-room door. She'd leave! She wouldn't live under the same roof with such an unfair person! And anyway, what had all that had to do with the business she'd come indoors to discuss?

She shook her head and went across the hall into the kitchen. The air was aromatic with the good smell of beef stew and there was a pleasant tang of apples, as well. Even as she watched, Mrs. Bennett took another pie from the oven and carried it to her work-table to cool. The smells and the sight of the pies helped, as did Mrs. Bennett's wise and understanding grin, her amiable "Hi."

Sighing, Laura sat down. "I suppose you heard?"

"I heard. You get too excited, Laura. He never mentioned Brad. You did."

Laura thought gloomily that that was true. "I just beat him to it, that was all."

"Maybe so, maybe not. How many pies did you want to take to the meeting?"

"As many as you can spare. Mrs. Bennett, why does he dislike Brad?"

"I always mind my own business, Laura. That's why I've been with you for ten years. You can take four pies. Your father's a fine man, by the way. Maybe his ideas and your ideas aren't the same, but he wants you to be happy, the same as you do."

And that, Laura supposed, was also true. But she did wish that just once he'd remember that she was over twenty and that a girl over twenty could think fairly intelligently, too. If she'd fallen head over heels in love with Brad just like that, her father might be justified in thinking as he did. But she'd not been an impulsive, overly emotional young idiot. Why, she'd known Brad for years! She'd had ample time to see Brad as he was. And what was he? Well, if he wasn't perfect he was as close to perfection as any young fellow could be. He worked. He planned. He saved. See what he'd already done with that run-down farm he'd inherited from his grandfather. And that was merely a beginning. Why, if he had a real chance, some decent capital behind him . . .

"You going to finish that yard, Laura? If not, you better put the tools away."

Oh, well, Laura thought, it would work out. Brad loved her and she loved him, and that was the big thing. As for an old-fashioned man who thought the twentieth century was the nineteenth century, he'd learn soon enough that it wasn't. In the meantime there was the yard to finish, dressing and eating to do, a meeting of the Flowers for Beauty Club to attend. And a kiss from Brad later on.

Laura's gray eyes sparkled. A quick, graceful figure in jeans and a wool work-shirt, she gave Mrs. Bennett a merry wave and hastened out to finish the yard work.

CHAPTER 2

Over George Washington Square in the dusk the offending sign blazed with a garish stridency. STALEY HOTEL, it read, FINE ROOMS, FINE FOOD. You could hear the sign's neon tubing sizzle and crackle and buzz. You could hear the sign itself creak on its brackets high above the street. There was still another sound, but Laura couldn't identify it as she strolled along the street en route to the Women's Club House in Saunder's Bluff Common. The sound was a shrill peeping sound of piercing intensity. It came intermittently, and never from the same place, and with varying degrees of volume. Interested and baffled, Laura stopped near the barber shop's plate-glass window for a careful exploration of the sky. She wondered if the sign were about to blow a fuse. She hated to seem disloyal to her own father, but a segment of her mind strongly wished the sign would go off forever. How hideous the colors were! What an eyesore to establish there in the business heart of the town!

The barber-shop door creaked open behind her. Old Mr. O'Neil stepped out to the sidewalk, a frail man in his white tunic, the walking equivalent of a newspaper. "Evening," he twanged. "That sound you hear is a bat." He pointed, and it was a bat, a little fellow that seemed almost too small to be alone in the great outdoors. "Been reading about them lately," Mr. O'Neil confided. "Seems Nature gave 'em a radar system. Those peeps they make are bounced back to 'em by anything solid and that's why, blind though they are, they never bump into anything. Interesting?"

"Very."

Laura's mind went on guard. When it came to gossip Mr. O'Neil was a pack rat. When he gave you something he expected to take something away.

"Nothing's more interesting than nature," Mr. O'Neil declared. "These bored kids who never know what to do with themselves should develop an interest in nature. If you use your eyes and ears and mind, you're never bored. There's always something worth looking at, worth thinking about."

"Was Brad in, Mr. O'Neil?"

Mr. O'Neil teetered to and fro on the practiced balls of his feet. "People are part of nature," he opined. "Stands to reason. Nature's just another word for God. Nature made us all, God made us all — it's the same thing. You study people and you aren't ever bored, either."

"Well, if you see him will you tell him to pick me up at the Club?"

"Take the fuss," Mr. O'Neil continued, "a lot of folks are making about that sign. Very interesting. I hear it, I think about it. I wonder what all the fuss is about. I wonder what the motives of those fussing people are."

Laura did the practical thing. She set the box of pies down on the sidewalk. She then leaned back against the brown-shingled wall of the old hotel and gazed speculatively at his wrinkled face. "Actually," she confessed, "I knew nothing about all the fuss until this afternoon."

"Yes, you don't come this way often, do you? Seems a shame, and your father so anxious to have you in the business."

"I'm afraid I'm a home girl, you see. I can't say I'm ashamed to be one, either. I think a great many girls who work at careers would gladly abandon those careers if they could. I've been lucky, very lucky, in that I've never been under the compulsion to work. Home's nice. I love to cook, to sew, to garden, to decorate — things like that. Oh, I use my intellect, too, Mr. O'Neil, much more often than you might suppose. But unfortunately for Dad, when I do think I think in terms of a husband and babies, home and my home town."

Laura paused.

Her contralto voice, soft and rich, then announced unequivocally: "I'm not ashamed of that, either."

Mr. O'Neil contemplated the clear May sky. A down-turned crescent moon was visible off toward the east. It shone with a hard yellow glitter, as did the generous sprinkling of stars visible wherever he glanced. "Stars don't move around the earth," he stated, "did you know? I like to pick up little things like that. I'm never bored. Take now. Right now the earth is streaking through space at maybe 50,000 miles an hour. Me, you, we're streaking right along with it. That's pretty interesting to me. But even more interesting to me is this: where are we going, Laura, huh?"

"To a home, to a husband, to babies, to a good life, perhaps."

So vigorously it surprised her he said: "No — not with Brad, at any rate."

"Why not?"

"I'll tell you about that sign," Mr. O'Neil twanged nasally. "That sign's really a pretty smart feller named Mr. Robert Staley working day and night to give his only child real security."

He broke off because now other people

could be observed coming along George Washington Square. Two youngsters, chattering feverishly, hustled by en route to a Friday evening movie at the Rivoli. Behind them came several fellows who wanted haircuts. They smiled at Laura and she returned the compliment, and as they continued into Mr. O'Neil's barber-shop she stooped and picked up her box of pies to stroll on toward the Women's Club House in the Common.

Mr. O'Neil sighed. "I like home girls," he confided. "I like home girls better, though, if they know what they're up against. I'll tell Brad you'll wait for him at the Club."

A little breeze sprang up as Laura walked by her father's old and comfortably prosperous hotel. It cooled her cheeks, which had grown hot for some reason that was inexplicable to her. It fluffed her curly black hair. She was annoyed about that and wished that she'd worn a hat or a scarf or a hairnet or something. The older ladies of the Club were always so critical of their juniors, and now that she was assistant chairwoman of the Purchasing Division of the Society, their criticisms would have bite. There was the penalty of high office. Resentment was born the instant you got a job the older ladies thought you were too young to hold, and that resentment was expressed in so many ways. Mrs. Plunkett was sure to mention that when *she'd* been a child proper female children had religiously worn hats. And Mrs. Plunkett's noble cohort and stanch ally Mrs. Coberly was certain to add —

Laura stopped short, laughing. She made a pretense of staring and blinking and staring again; as if startled and very surprised. She was so pert and saucy then, with the breeze fluttering her skirt and tousling her hair, that Brad, who'd blocked her path, actually laughed.

"Ah," he laughed, "you're not that surprised, honey. You knew darned well I was alive all the time."

"I did?"

"And why did you come this way if you didn't half expect to see me? The other way's shorter."

"Perhaps I longed to see the new hotel sign. My, my, what a big opinion you have of yourself."

"If you'll close your mouth," he bribed, "I'll kiss it."

"Brad Holbrook!"

"Laura Staley!"

She was so astounded she did stop speaking and he did kiss her mouth — and with gusto.

Behind them someone laughed.

Blushing, trembling, Laura peered over her

shoulder, and wished that she hadn't. Mrs. Plunkett gave an eloquent nod and shrug at her companion Mrs. Coberly, and the two ladies then ostentatiously crossed the road so as to avoid having to exchange evening greetings with a gamin.

Brad was perspicacity personified. "They don't like you," Brad said.

Laura dismissed them buoyantly. "It doesn't matter. Really it doesn't." She handed him the box of pies. She got her various emotions sorted out and studied the sky and wished they could make it a long evening date. Hang it all, why was she even a member of the Flowers for Beauty Society? The older ladies didn't want her. She was endured only because of her father. Why did she waste so darned much time on such unimportant things and unpleasant people?

"The reason I love you," Brad kidded, "is that you're a good conversationalist. Have you ever noticed that most girls just tag along beside you, saying nothing?"

"My, you are feeling sassy this evening! You actually laughed. You kissed me in public! You're teasing me. Has someone you hated died and left you ten cents?"

They reached the Common. Toward the Club House area the Common was nicely lighted, and they could see a dozen or so ladies dutifully following the several paths that led to the pleasant-looking white frame building. But off toward their left the Common was intriguingly dark and seemed deserted enough to give them privacy, and Brad led her in that direction and to a bench under the towering elms.

Laura pretended to be irritated. "You know, Brad, I happen to be an officer of the Society. We must all remember our duties."

"This'll take just a minute."

"Oh, grand! How delightfully romantic!"

He chuckled sheepishly, yet after they were seated on the bench under the soughing elms, he didn't reach for her hand nor did his lips come her way at once.

"It's business, honey," he explained. "We'll have to wait about the barn. Maybe we won't have much to do on it after all. That Miss Quinby's a good real-estate agent. You know what she did? She advertised that barn in even the New York City newspapers, and a guy named Albright came out yesterday and —"

"Albright? A big, very good-looking blond fellow?"

"Yup, that's the guy. Where'd you meet him?"

It was nice to know that Brad could be jealous. It was wonderful to feel she was that important to him.

"Well, this guy's a big-shot producer in New York City, honey. I don't know much about him myself, but he has a couple of hits playing on Broadway now, and Miss Quinby says this Albright and Julie Trotter are just like that. Anyway —"

"Gulp."

"Huh?"

"Why, he was practically standing in my yard. If I'd just shaken hands with him I could have told our great grandchildren that one May afternoon I touched the hand that had squeezing rights to Julie Trotter's."

"Will you stop joking?" Doggedly, Brad Holbrook plunged on. "What I'm trying to say is that this guy's thinking of putting a summer theater out here in my barn. He wants it on a five-year lease, though, for a thousand a year, and —"

"Brad, is this a joke?"

His laughter, boisterous and gay, was all the answer anyone could want.

Laura's scalp tingled. Why, they'd be rich! Brad netted two thousand a year easily from his farm. He made at least another two thousand net a year from his variety store, and if you added another thousand a year to all that, you had all the money you needed on which to marry, to raise a family!

"Glory," she whispered. "Glory."

At last his arm did go around her and he her close. "Not bad, Laura, huh? Not that money's everything, but it sure helps."

She shivered superstitiously. "Hush Brad. Glory, don't even think that way — do you want to queer it?"

"How can I queer it when the decision's up to me? Say, why do you think I was over there waiting for you to come along? I wanted to talk it over with you, see?"

"You mean all you have to do is sign a paper and the barn's rented?"

"Yup."

About to twist free, to get him to that paper in a hurry, Laura suddenly changed her mind. Had she fancied it, or had a different tone come into his voice? She gave his thin, tanned face a sidelong glance. Much of his face was obscured by the dark, but in the moonlight filtering down through the old elms she did catch a glimpse of his eyes. Abruptly, the elation surging through her came to a grinding pause.

"Go on, Brad." Her voice was cool and serious now, not the happy, proud, contented voice of a girl strongly and headlong in love. "What's the rest?"

"Look, Laura, these things don't always go the way you like. I mean, naturally, for a thousand dollars on that kind of lease, a man wants more than just an old barn. He wants things fixed up and cleaned up and kept that way. And he wants other kinds of help at least during his first season. You know, a thousand dollars is a lot of money for a barn in these parts."

"Go on."

"Well, I told him I'm engaged, that we were sort of figuring on being married maybe around the end of June."

"Brad!"

Brad got up. It was his constant claim he always thought better on his feet because he was on his feet so much. He paced away from the bench, he paced back toward the bench. "Well," he said tautly, "there was nothing definite. What I mean is, your Dad hadn't given permission and —"

"I told you that was unnecessary."

"To me it is. What sort of guy do you think I am? Do you think I'd want to come between you and your Dad? That would be light-minded, and I'm not light-minded."

"But I've explained —"

His voice rose and drowned out hers. It always did rise, she recalled, when he was in the wrong. Being in the wrong always made him furious.

"Another thing," he snapped, "is that I don't like him to say I'm keeping you from entering his business because I hope to force him to let me into it later on. I'm my own man. I don't want anything he has, and even if I did I wouldn't go after it that way. If you want to know, I think you ought to go in with him."

Laura went rigid. Her own temper rose, but she managed to ask, calmly enough: "But what has all this to do with the barn, Brad?"

"Well, I told this guy I'd talk to you. I told him about what we were figuring on doing, and that I didn't think it was right for me to take on that extra work and postpone our marriage until maybe this fall or winter or next spring."

"Or next century, Brad?"

"That's no way to talk!"

"It was to be this spring, remember? Then you hatched this barn idea. What am I supposed to do, cheer?"

"Look, am I rich? Can I afford to turn up my nose on such an easy five thousand dollars?"

"We could still be married. I could help you on the farm and —"

"No. You can yell or scream your head off, but I'm not taking you from that great big home and a servant to make a drudge of you. A fellow has his pride."

"Brad, will you just be sensible? Am I a

China doll or something? Do you think I'm incapable of working hard? Do you think I'd object to working hard?"

He was standing very close again, his lean figure tense, his hands twisting at his sides. "It's not what you think you want," he grated harshly; "it's what I feel is right for you. Look, with a little more money I can maybe make another good investment like that store. And with another investment like that paying off — well, I just thought you should know."

"In other words, it isn't what I want, but what you want?"

"It's what's sensible. Laura, will you just think it over? You'll see how right I am."

But he wasn't, Laura thought feverishly. He was wrong.

"Anyway, Laura, that's the whole proposition. I say I should grab it and let marriage wait. It'll be nicer anyway when I'm not so busy."

"Brad, I wish you'd understand I wouldn't object to the work. It would be the two of us working together. Brad, it would be glorious. It'd be fun!"

A blunder!

He shook his head and sighed. "Ah, stop being a kid, Laura. What do you know about being poor, or working hard? I say in six months you'd be fed up and want to go back to your Dad. Only feeling as he does about me now, he wouldn't take you back if you married me. Then what?"

"Brad, he doesn't hate you. He thinks that —"

"Skip it."

"Brad!"

"I've got things to do and you've got a meeting to attend. And what's the point of arguing? A poor man needs money, and I have the chance to make some money, and there it is."

Nor would he discuss it further. He took her arm and all but hauled her from the bench, and led her through the moonlit dark to the lighted section near the Club House. There he studied the appearance she made in her hundred-dollar gray wool suit and her hundred-and-fifty-dollar cashmere coat. "Oh, sure," he said. "Being poor would suit you fine."

He turned and strode away. Laura, her gray eyes dilating, watched him and wanted to run after him. Then Belle Adrian saw her and came running down the Club House steps. "You're just in time, dear. As you know, we're expected to submit our rose-bush planting scheme to the full meeting this evening. But what about the cost? I'm told at the last minute that it will be prohibitive."

Gloomily, Laura went into the Club House

with her. The first person she saw in the little lobby was Mrs. Plunkett, and Mrs. Plunkett came over, her eyes glittering, not missing a detail. "My goodness," Mrs. Plunkett declared, "your hair *is* a sight, isn't it? Now when I was a child proper female children religiously wore hats. Nor were we, if I may say it, Laura, such uninhibited creatures as the girls of your generation seem to be."

"Dear Mrs. Plunkett," Belle Adrian said nervously, "you must excuse us. A very important detail has been overlooked, and perhaps there's still time for the Purchasing Division to rise nobly, like an army, as it were, to the occasion."

Mrs. Plunkett gave a properly democratic presidential nod. "Certainly, Mrs. Adrian, certainly."

Laura tagged along reluctantly. What was the point of doing anything, she wondered, when you couldn't even marry the fellow you loved?

CHAPTER 3

Early in the freshness and pinkness of dawn, Laura got out of bed and put on her work clothes and work cap. She had a quick breakfast of apple-pie and milk in the kitchen. She thought she was being very quiet, a considerate young lady indeed. But as she crossed the back yard to get her Ford out of the garage, a second-story window opened and her father's semi-bald head came into view. "I want to talk to you," he growled. "Wait in the study, please."

It would involve business and Brad again, she imagined, and it would be a waste of his time and hers. She tried shaking her head regretfully. It accomplished nothing. "I said wait in the study," her father snapped, and she had no choice but to obey.

In the study, waiting for him to come downstairs, she sat as usual in the green leather armchair and surveyed the oil portrait of her mother. She had few memories of her mother. She had a vague recollection of a happy chuckle and she was sure that her mother had used a lavender scent because whenever she smelled lavender in the air it brought her mother into her mind. But there was little else in her memory to humanize the lovely face hanging eternally on the knotty-pine wall.

Clumps in the hall, and the door swung open. "Well, Laura, sleep well?" Mr. Robert Staley, a smiling, well-rested father, came across the study for his due. Laura dutifully kissed the proffered cheek.

"Dad, I hope it's important. I'm helping Brad with his barn. Isn't it wonderful, Dad? Brad's rented his barn for five years at a thousand dollars a year."

He fluttered a hand. "Yes. I know. In fact, Mayor Wolfe and I discussed the matter very thoroughly last evening." He paused and shrugged. He added dryly: "Among other things, of course."

"It'll be fun, Dad, won't it? Imagine having a summer theater right here in Saunder's Bluff! Beautiful women! Handsome, dashing young men! Golly, won't the old town hum?"

Her father achieved his goal — the swivel chair behind the desk. "Inevitably," he said, "Brad Holbrook joined the conference. He seemed distraught."

Laura turned back to the window. It was good strategy, she'd long ago learned, never to give him a good look at her face at such times. "He was?" she asked politely.

"Bah." He was contemptuous. He sat stiffly on his chair, his gray brows knit above his short, full nose, his lips drawn tightly into a frown. "It wasn't necessary for him to tell me that once again the marriage would have to be postponed. It's all a part of his strategy."

Laura whirled. "Understand this, Dad: I didn't wait here to argue. The truth is there's nothing to be gained by argument. You disapprove of Brad. Just why, I don't know. Brad's everything young men are supposed to be — he's industrious, he's serious, he's decent. Still, you disapprove. So whenever you can you attack his motives — apparently because there's nothing else to attack. Well, it's a matter of opinion, and my opinion just isn't yours."

It was as if she'd not spoken. Robert Staley continued: "Naturally, I'm cognizant of his strategy. Because I'm concerned about your security, he affects the same concern. Because I state you're entitled to decent comfort, he nobly states he won't marry you until he can offer that decent comfort. Now I know and he knows that he will be unable to provide what I call decent comfort. It's a simple matter of arithmetic. However, he does possess one small advantage — the fact that you imagine you're in love with him."

"I am!"

"And so nobly, very properly, he postpones again and again. In the meantime you subject me to a certain pressure. In the meantime my business affairs subject me to a certain pressure. And the end result will be what, he thinks? Why, that one day the pressure will cause me to give your marriage my blessing — and to invite *him* to enter my business."

Laura gasped, deeply and genuinely shocked. "Dad, how can you even think such horrid things? For shame!"

"I simply thought you should know."

"I should *know?*"

His rather full face reddened. He stirred restlessly, glanced out the window at the sky. "I'm not deaf, Laura. Nor am I stupid. I can hear a girl crying, even softly, in the night. I can link cause with effect. And perhaps, although I must seem hardhearted and arbitrary and arrogant to you at times, I'm just human enough to want my daughter to know she's crying, really, for something that doesn't exist in Brad."

Laura swallowed. But the doorbell rang and startled and distracted her. She glanced peevishly at her wristwatch, wondering who in the world was calling at that hour of the morning. Yet she welcomed the interruption because it gave her an opportunity to leave without seeming to be retreating. She swung the front door open just as the big fellow with the shock of golden hair was about to press the bell button a second time. It was an effort, but she managed to smile back at him cordially. "Oh, it's Mr. Albright. How nice. Won't you come in, Mr. Albright?"

"Ken will do, Miss Staley. And actually I've come to give Holbrook a hand. He's involved with pigs or chickens or some such thing, and I drove in to pick you up."

She didn't hesitate. She promptly stepped out onto the porch and closed the door firmly behind her. So it had been just another spat? Brad *had* expected her and wanted her after all? The knowledge sent a current of warmth tingling through her. She developed a definite affection for Mr. Ken Albright as she hurried down the brick path to Brad's car parked at the curb. Such a grand and handsome bearer of good tidings! "It was pigs," she said after she'd gotten seated. "At this hour of the day Brad's always involved with his pigs."

"Strange beasties. I spent the night with Brad at the farm. About two this morning I was awakened by a rumbling sound and the house seemed to be shaking. It was a pig scratching his side against the house just outside my window."

Now the full sun, an effulgent purple-red, broke through the low-lying clouds in the east. All the earth seemed to turn red and shiny. Windows sparkled, dew sparkled, the road was a blaze spread before them. Now the mountains in the west came clearly and majestically to the eye. They weren't great mountains nor especially wild-looking mountains, but their wooded slopes and folds and crannies, their beautifully rondured peaks, their air of being half of earth and half of sky, lent them a very majestic distinction. Laura was stirred by the sight. Somewhat gauchely she asked: "Have you ever seen more impressive mountains, Mr. Albright?"

"They're quite beautiful, aren't they?"

"A long time ago, when this nation was younger than he was, one of my ancestors shot a bear up in those mountains. So he wrote, at least, in his diary."

They drove along Franklin D. Roosevelt Avenue into George Washington Square. The business heart of Saunder's Bluff was still with a weekend stillness, only a couple of men being visible, only birds making any sound.

"A very peaceful community," Ken Albright said approvingly. "I may as well say I wasn't especially optimistic when I first saw Saunder's Bluff. I couldn't imagine so small and quiet a community supporting the type of summer theater I envisage. However, Miss Quinby persuaded me to go for a drive with her, and I changed my mind. There are certainly enough people in the area, and you're close enough to large cities to —"

"And there are vacationists, Mr. Albright. Not that we in Saunder's Bluff bother much with the tourist trade, but for miles around there are all sorts of tourist resorts and vacation hotels. I should estimate your potential audience during the summer would easily exceed a hundred and fifty thousand."

He was quick, it developed, and he had a sense of humor. "Oh," he said lightly, "I've already been sold, Miss Staley. The papers were signed last evening, and I'm committed."

Her heart drummed. "How nice!"

And on they drove, passing through the area of small shops and the Common and coming to another residential district. Now the trees on each side of the road were elms, the houses were smaller, the yard plantings were less ambitious and ostentatious. It was in this area that the Flowers for Beauty Society intended to work, and as a good Club member should, Laura conscientiously scrutinized the chosen terrain. Her opinion then, as it had been last evening, as it had been for weeks, was that the idea of planting rosebushes was a poor one. The bushes would be expensive. The work of upkeep would be heavy. Moreover, she thought, there'd be no quick color, no —

"How many factories around here, Miss Staley?"

"Five or six. Of course, the big one is the optical company. They manufacture field glasses, binoculars, microscopes, lenses for eyeglasses. We're very pleased with the Woglom Optical Company because theirs isn't seasonal work, and there aren't any layoffs for retooling, things like that."

"The reason I asked, you see, is that one of my staff in New York thinks we could ensure a fairly good house by offering season tickets at a discount to the factory workers. Think it would interest any of them?"

Now they drove over the bridge spanning Corkscrew Creek. The water was so clear you could count the stones lying on the bottom. Laura thought she saw a fish but wasn't sure because before she could check they'd reached the opposite shore.

"I imagine," she guessed, "that you'd sell a number of tickets. It used to be, I'm told, that factory workers were disinterested in any form of culture. Nowadays, though, everyone seems to be interested in just about everything. We draw a good crowd during the summer to the band concerts in the Common."

"Well, we'll give it a whirl. Incidentally,

if I'm asking too many questions, don't hesitate to say so. But I ought to add at this point that your interests are involved, too. Inevitably, business at your hotel will boom. And Holbrook tells me your father has several motels scattered about and a few other interests to boot."

Laura blinked. For the first time it occurred to her that naturally the establishment of a summer theater in the area would increase business in general and cause many changes. The town would fill up with playgoers, sightseers. If the summer theater were a success the town would undergo a boom. Would it be good for the town? What would happen to the pleasant, easy way of life they all enjoyed there?

"Or doesn't money interest you, Miss Staley?"

"I've not thought about money very often. At least in connection with myself."

"So Holbrook's told me."

They'd reached the highway at last. The car began to move ahead at a brisker pace. Gradually the scene changed. The land, the sky impinged more sharply upon Laura's awareness, and the fresh beauty of the morning and the world around her brought a happy smile to her lips. "I prefer this," she said simply. "And if you must know, Mr. Albright,

I'm a girl who's sorry she didn't come to this country several hundred years ago, when it was still as God made it."

"Take the world as it is," he suggested. "I always do. Leave the what-might-have-beens to dispensers of illusions such as I."

It was about time! Another two minutes, Laura thought, and she'd have raised *that* subject herself. "It must be exciting to be in the theater, Mr. Albright. All those beautiful women, all those handsome young men — and such glamour and excitement!"

His blue eyes twinkled. "Oh, my," he teased, "we are inexperienced, aren't we? My dear Miss Staley, there's only one word for the theater, and that's work. As, of course, you'll have the opportunity to discover for yourself this summer."

"Is she as beautiful as they say, Mr. Albright?"

"I beg your pardon?"

"Julie Trotter, I mean. I almost saw her once. It was in Boston. A friend and I were leaving our hotel, and someone said, 'There's Julie Trotter!' and we looked — just in time to see her pumps getting into a cab."

He laughed, and there was a nice bounce in his tones and a warm, satisfactory male vibrato. Queerly, the laugh made him a human being to her, not merely the handsome face he'd been until then.

"I must tell Julie that," he said. "Of course you'll meet her this summer. Ours will be a repertory company, Miss Staley. Somewhat experimental, but not so experimental as to incline the Revenue Department's tax collectors to believe my motive for establishing this theater is to run up a tax loss. I think there will be guest stars, and if that's so I'm positive Julie will be one of them."

"How wonderful!"

There it was up the road, the farm Brad had inherited from his grandfather and which he was operating alone now that his parents had settled down in faraway California. The sight of the farm drove all theater talk from Laura's mind. The theater was make-believe, but a working farm in rural Vermont was an exciting, satisfying reality. She loved the stone fences; she loved the old trees. She loved the fields spread under the golden sun, the quaint farmhouse, the well-house, the outbuildings, the huge weathered barn. For an instant it gave her a pang to think of that barn performing a function it had never been designed to perform. But a trick of her vision wrote a thousand dollars across the face of the barn, and now her heart began to drum in earnest.

"It should work out nicely, Mr. Albright. Brad could make an opening in the fence over there, and you could have a nice parking area built and perhaps plant a few small trees and shrubs and gain a wonderfully picturesque effect."

He drove in through the gate and parked the car before the quaint, two-story, steeply roofed farmhouse. It wasn't necessary for him to beep the horn. Brad came out, wiping his hands on a dish-towel and grinning from ear to ear. "Hi," he said, and there was no tension in his voice, no residue of the anger he'd expressed last night. "Great morning, Laura, isn't it?"

She got out of the car and turned to look in all directions.

"Laura," Brad said, "Albright and I got a lot of things to talk over with you. I guess he told you the lease has been signed."

"Uh-huh." Then, to make sure he understood that she honestly did approve, she added: "I think it's wonderful, too, Brad. It'll be good for all the merchants in town, won't it?"

"There." Brad sat down, triumph on his lean, tanned face. His shining brown eyes bored into Ken Albright's blue ones. "It's like I told you, Albright. Everybody with common sense will say it's a good thing. Laura's got common sense, and what she's said proves it. Sure, Mr. Staley will fuss and yell a little, but he sure can't stop this, believe me."

"Stop this?" Laura squinted through the sunshine at Brad's face and then, just like that, her heart stopped its happy thumping. A feeling of disappointment, annoyance, stabbed through her. Then he'd not really expected her. He'd sent Mr. Albright after her because her father was kicking up a fuss and because it had seemed logical to get her to help them.

Ken Albright said quietly: "He opposes the whole idea on the grounds it will destroy much that is good in Saunder's Bluff. And he seems to have Mayor Wolfe behind him. Holbrook's thought was that possibly you could make him understand he'd benefit more than most would."

"I see."

Laura went up to the porch and sat down in one of the old wicker chairs. Although she'd gotten some sleep last night after the tears had stopped, she suddenly felt very, very tired. She was tired of being disappointed. She was tired of waiting. But more than that, she was tired of a love that asked for so much and gave so little back in return.

Brad seemed unaware of that tiredness, however. "Say," Brad exclaimed, "let's get in the house. Albright's drawn up some plans that'll interest you."

Laura ignored that. She looked up at the

handsome face of Ken Albright. "Can my Dad stop you?"

"No, of course not. He can cause us a certain inconvenience, however. For instance, it was my assumption that because of the extra business our enterprise would attract to Saunder's Bluff he'd — well, he'd give me a cut rate for my troupe at the hotel."

"I see."

"Laura," Brad said excitedly, "sure you'll help. Why, if this thing's as big as it looks, I'll make money in more ways than you can skin a cat. That's important, isn't it?"

Ah, yes, Laura thought, Money.

"Well," she said gently, "let's deal with one thing at a time, Brad, shall we?"

CHAPTER 4

Laura hurried across the parking-lot to Vermont Court. She found a little breeze there, surprisingly, and she halted under one of the birch trees to cool off and to get her strategy figured out.

Then she strode on, a young, lovely sight in her light gray skirt and yellow cashmere sweater. When she reached the two-story brick building at the foot of Vermont Court she superstitiously crossed her fingers, drew a deep breath, then forced a brightly confident smile to her lips and went inside.

Promptly, the receptionist frowned. "I don't know, Miss Laura," she said. "Your father's very busy."

"Don't be so pessimistic, Teddy. Just get him on that thingamajig and tell him I'm leaving for Europe at four. If that doesn't work tell him Mrs. Bennett has quit. *That* ought to work!"

Teddy chuckled. She got Mr. Staley on the intercom system and dutifully gave him the message.

There was a long silence, then a resigned sigh. "Oh, send her in, Teddy. And will you get hold of Williston at the hotel and inform him I'm dissatisfied with this month's receipts?"

"Yes, sir."

Laura pushed through the swinging door at the far end of the reception room and nodded at her father's secretary, Mrs. Staunton. Mrs. Staunton nodded back. "You won't be long, dear, will you? Your father is having a conference with Mr. King at two."

"Just a few minutes, Mrs. Staunton. Incidentally, if you have a few spare minutes this weekend, would you mind checking up on the prices Sears, Roebuck is asking for rosebushes?"

"The whole idea is preposterous. I've said it at the Club and I say it again. The proper thing for us to do is to make a large purchase of seeds and inexpensive plants. We should then advertise in the *Clarion* that these seeds and plants will be given free to anyone who will agree to plant them in his front yard and along the curbs."

"In Mrs. Plunkett's considered opinion —"

"Humph!"

They were interrupted by Mr. Staley, who'd obviously grown impatient. He stuck his head into Mrs. Staunton's office and growled: "Well, Laura, I can't wait all day."

It would be a fine battle, she thought, a real sizzler.

The sun came out as she stepped into his large, plainly furnished office. It was weak sunlight, a tremulous yellow, but it was a welcome sight after two days of gray and threatening weather. It inspirited Laura. It seemed to light up the dark and moody crannies of her mind, and her forced smile became a genuine smile as she perched on a corner of her father's desk.

He noticed that and nodded. "About time," he growled, "that you became yourself. About time a lot of other people became themselves, too. I've had ten telephone calls this morning about that ridiculous theater project. Several were downright rude. I was actually accused of deliberately attempting to interfere with the natural and normal development of this town. Why? Well, the explanation was that since I'm making money, I'm content with the town as it is."

"Aren't you?"

He sat down. He made a fist, and he banged that fist on the desk. "A good healthy skepticism would do a lot of dreamers good. I blame Bowser of the *Clarion* as much as anyone else. Did you read that article of his yesterday morning?"

Laura had. Like her father, she had felt that

Mr. Bowser had crossed the bridge to success before the bridge had even been built. But she knew better than to admit as much.

"They'll calm down," she predicted. "Naturally, enthusiastic people are inclined to see just the bright side of things. Mr. Albright and his troupe have a lot of work to do. And the renovation of that barn has just begun. By the time the theater opens and the first play is produced a lot of people will have cooled off and done some real thinking, and then —"

His eyes, very steely suddenly, stopped her cold.

"You seem very sure the theater will open, Laura."

"I'm sure."

"I don't suppose you'd care to elaborate?"

"Why not? This is the twentieth century, not the nineteenth. While you're a very important man in this community, Dad, you're just one man. The most you could do would be to force a vote. The vote would go against you, and the theater would open anyway."

"Perhaps the delay would discourage Mr. Albright."

"I doubt it. The lease has been signed, as Mr. Bowser reported. He'd have to pay the thousand a year even if he never established his summer theater here. So, of course, the delay might inconvenience him but it wouldn't stop him."

He nodded. He settled back in his chair. He drummed his fingertips on the desk.

Laura decided that toughness would be unnecessary.

"Dad, do you have five minutes to give me — my personal affairs, that is?"

He did something that warmed her to her toes. There was no hesitancy. He was up and across the room almost before she'd finished speaking. He poked his head out into Mrs. Staunton's office and snapped: "Tell King I'll see him tomorrow. And if I have other appointments, please cancel them."

Mrs. Staunton was incredulous. "Sir?"

Mr. Staley merely closed the door. He gave Laura's working face a shrewd stare, then shrugged and returned to his desk. The chair creaked under him, and he sighed. "I should have assistance here. There are many details that should be handled by someone else. I would then have the time to devote to more important matters. It isn't economical or efficient for a hundred-dollar man to deal with a ten-dollar problem."

Laura understood what he was trying to do: that he was giving her time to assemble her thoughts. Her lips curled in an affectionate smile. "You're not entirely hopeless, Pop," she teased. "You have kind and generous instincts, haven't you?"

"Perhaps you had better wait," he countered dryly, "until after you have finished. It involves Brad Holbrook, doesn't it?"

"Understand, Pop, will you, that I do love him and that I am sure he loves me? This has nothing to do with any doubts involving Brad or myself. Okay?"

He clasped his hands and pursed his lips.

Laura went on, putting into expression certain of the thoughts that had troubled her ever since last Saturday. "But I will concede, Pop, that for a man in love Brad is reluctant to marry. It's strange, but I never quite realized how reluctant he is until I was discussing the theater plans with him last Saturday. He'd disappointed me again, much more severely, Pop, than you'll ever guess."

"No." His face was less stern now, was as gentle and kind, in fact, as she'd ever seen it. "I'm not exactly insensitive, Laura. And I've always given you credit for believing sincerely that Brad Holbrook is important to you. I understood the disappointment was severe."

Her gray eyes flashed suddenly. "Perhaps I've allowed Brad to take me for granted. They say that's poor technique. Technique! Who wants to maneuver a man into marrying her? Still . . . well, he does seem to think only his convenience matters and — well, I don't like that."

"Well . . ."

Laura stood up. She'd come to the point after many hours of feverish thinking at home in her bed. But now that she had come to the point she was hesitant to continue. Perhaps she was being foolish. Perhaps this wasn't the way, either. And yet, what else was there to do? Perhaps if Brad were jolted he'd understand that the important thing wasn't that money he was forever chasing but the girl he presumably loved.

She drove herself on. "Well, the point is that I'm tired of sitting at home, waiting for Brad to suit his convenience. I thought that possibly you'd give me a job, and that probably I should see less of Brad."

"Certainly. Gladly." Mr. Staley grew so excited at this point he leapt to his feet and his eyes began to shine.

"I thought the hotel would be interesting, Pop. If we were to make a special rate for the Albright Players, the hotel would need an extra worker. Fair enough?"

His brows came together. He understood, all right, and it was apparent he disliked it. "That way," he said, "you'd be helping Brad, eh? The end of my opposition, and all that?"

"Everyone would be helped, Dad, if you'd

support the new project as you should. The town could use the extra business the theater would attract."

He sat down again, and in a twinkling became the conservative business-man who wanted to study all the angles and possibilities.

"Suppose I think about it?" he asked.

Laura nodded and smiled, feeling happier now that she had put her thoughts into words and was engaged in something other than morbid stewing.

"Sure, Pop. You might remember this, though: that if I did take a job with you I'd not quit for anything less than marriage. Fair enough?"

It told.

She knew as she left that that was what he'd been waiting to hear.

Out in the Court she did one thing more. She removed the engagement ring from her finger and stuffed it into the pocket of her skirt. Then, quickly, her lovely head high, a pleasant smile on her young, lovely face, she went back to the Ford in the parking-lot.

CHAPTER 5

In New York City, toward the middle of May, Ken Albright was agreeably surprised. "Either there's a gimmick," he said, "or she loves that bumpkin more intensely than she should."

Manny Cohen drawled: "She loves him. Incidentally, fellow, you should try to develop a certain respect for the human race. You should always assume that whatever anyone does is done for decent, laudable reasons."

Ken laughed but without mirth. "Raise your wages, Manny. What I should do is give you a spot in a play. You're a funnier comedian than several stars I could name."

Manny made a long arm and snapped his thumb and forefinger imperiously. "Give."

Ken gave him the neatly typed letter. He then got up and strolled down the center aisle toward the doors standing open to the lobby. The sour, soggy air of the theater depressed him. He had an urge to return to Vermont, to resume his inevitable investigation of the streets and courts of Saunder's Bluff. For some reason he didn't particularly understand, he had a special desire to see James Monroe Street again as he had seen it in the mellow glow of perfect spring sunshine. He wondered how many of the bumpkins who dwelt on that street appreciated its beauty, its quaint old-world charm. Laura Staley did, of course. That was clear enough. But the others?

Out in the lobby, Frank Jones grinned and weakly waved. Frank's round, red face was beaded with perspiration. Frank's collar had wilted. Frank's suit was so limp and wrinkled it looked as if it had been slept in. He was a mess, Ken thought, not without distaste, but he was indispensable to the Albright organization, just as Manny Cohen was. What Frank didn't know about acting and stage technique wasn't worth knowing. He was a good fellow to have around because he wasn't temperamental and he wasn't greedy.

"Lovely day, boss."

"Lovely."

Frank studied the big fellow, and there was awe in Frank's eyes. The big fellow looked as if he'd just stepped from his house, perfectly dressed and groomed for the day. His creamy-tan gabardine suit was spotless, unwrinkled. Every hair on his head was in place; his face was a fresh pink that seemed untroubled by anything, the soggy warm weather included.

"Dear boss," said Frank, "will you tell a mere mortal how you do it?"

Ken grimaced, in no mood for nonsense. "I thought the rehearsal was scheduled for ten."

Frank flipped his cigarette out to the street. It was a gray and shabby street, not as crowded or busy or noisy as it usually was. "I canceled it," Frank said. "I said to myself I'd hate to work in weather like this, and so I canceled the rehearsal forthwith."

Ken grunted. He didn't feel like arguing, but it seemed to him that he owed it to his position to make a protest. "Wasn't that exceeding your authority?"

Frank didn't bat an eye. "A director has some authority, or so I'm told."

"I was particularly anxious to put Julie's understudy through her paces. She handles the drama nicely. The lighter scenes, however, are elephantine."

"At which point," said Frank, "I would like to make a point. That point is this, Ken. You're a good producer. You aren't afraid to spend money to make money. You aren't afraid to experiment. You aren't afraid to work with unknowns. So you have two hits going, and you've not had a flop since you got into this racket, and if you don't end up a millionaire a dozen times over I'll miss my guess. But you don't know acting. And since you're paying me big money to handle that end of it, why don't you let me handle it?"

"That's blunt enough."

"But I love you just the same." Frank grinned. "I love you deeply because you're the only fellow I know who'll risk important money on a pair of fives. No offense intended, Ken."

Yes, Ken thought, that was true, too. When Frank had a point to make he made it without rancor, without unpleasantness. He spoke his mind, as a fellow should. Probably that was why he got along so well with Frank. Probably that was why the Albright Players didn't run into the difficulties other groups did. Frank was an easy going guy you couldn't help but like despite his penchant for speaking the truth as he saw it.

It was a good organization, Ken mused. Perhaps he'd better drop the rehearsal issue on the spot.

He did. "Well," he smiled, "you're worth your pay, Frank. You're not worth more, but you are worth that. But just between us, man to man, are you satisfied with Sylvia's handling of the lighter scenes?"

"Nope."

"Well, then?"

"But you can't have it two ways, Ken. You can't drag me out to the bugs and pumpkins and have me supervising things here, too. So if I'm going out to moo with the cows Julie has to stay here and give her all for the vacationists."

Ken winced.

Manny came out, grinning, rubbing his hands briskly. "Great. Speaking as a business-manager, I say it's wonderful. But how did you wangle the cut rate at that hotel, Ken? I thought you said the old fellow who owns the hotel was against you."

"I didn't. The credit should go to Brad Holbrook, if to anyone. Apparently he convinced Miss Staley that she owed it to him to work on her father. Well, there it is, Manny. I think her offer is fair enough, don't you?"

"Obviously."

"Well, then, it should work out. We won't make any money to speak of this season, the costs of renovation and all that considered. But it'll cut our taxes for this year, and probably next year we'll make a nice bundle up in Vermont. Work it out and give me the figures by tomorrow, Manny, will you?"

"Can do."

"Oh, and do we have one of Julie's pictures lying around?"

Frank snickered. "By a curious coincidence, boss, we have a thousand."

"Well, I'll take one with me. This may jolt

you worldly, cynical creatures, but Miss Staley is still excited because once upon a time she caught a glimpse of Julie's shoes getting into a cab. An autographed picture sent her by Julie herself ought to be a nice, inexpensive way of thanking Miss Staley."

Frank wagged his head. Very respectfully he said: "I apologize, boss. You won't end up with a couple of million — you'll end up with a billion in cash."

Amused, with the picture in his brief-case, Ken got into a cab ten minutes later and rode downtown to Greenwich Village and West Eleventh Street. As he alighted from the cab the gray, low-hanging clouds released the first of the rain that had been prophesied by the weather bureau. The drops were very light and "feathery," and Ken felt oddly frustrated as he swung open the wrought-iron gate in Julie's wrought-iron fence. Blast it, he thought, why didn't it really rain? Perhaps a good rain would break the heat, the humidity. Perhaps then New York City would be tolerable once more.

Disgruntled, he went up the shallow steps of the stoop and rang the doorbell of the three-story, brown-stone front. While he stood waiting for Julie's maid to answer, he made certain decisions about Julie. The first was that of course she would have to remain in the play during most of the summer. Frank's point had been well taken. Frank would be required in Vermont, and obviously they couldn't jeopardize the good business they were doing in New York by putting an inadequate understudy into Julie's role and permitting her to work unsupervised. No, taking Julie to Vermont was out. And another thing was —

The door opened and broke his train of thought. It was Julie herself, a very satisfactory sight in a light, peach-colored hostess gown that gave her the interesting appearance of being very demure and fragile. Julie held out both her hands. Gaily, she smiled. "Angry, dearest? Never be angry, Ken. We live, we make money, all life is ours to enjoy, and what else matters?"

He thought as he stepped inside that Julie carried her own atmosphere of glamour wherever she went, that she was the one actress he knew who didn't require props or special clothes or carefully written lines to bring out the best of her. He tossed his hat to the refectory table in the hall and followed her into her spacious, comfortably air-conditioned living-room. "Oh," he told her, "it doesn't matter. As a matter of fact, Julie, Frank and I have decided you'd better remain in the play this summer."

Never a pause in her graceful progress to

the chesterfield, never a tremor of lips, of chin. She sat down and gaily waved him to his favorite chair near the candy-stone fireplace. "I think it will be a delightful storm, darling. I rather imagine the thunder will boom and the lightning will blaze and the rain will come down in torrents."

Julie's maid came in, trimly dressed in her white uniform. "Will you have breakfast now, Miss Trotter?"

Only then did Julie betray herself. "No, Hortense, I won't. I'm afraid that I've lost my appetite."

"But you must eat, Miss Trotter. The doctor said —"

"That will be all, Hortense. Oh, wait a moment, please. Ken, will you have iced coffee?"

"No, thanks." Ken glanced at his wristwatch. He had a lunch engagement at his club. He then had an appointment with the architect who'd drawn up the tentative plans for the summer theater. He had a problem there, too. He had the problem of talking the architect into going up to Saunder's Bluff to look over the barn and to give recommendations and suggestions — all at a cost that wouldn't be prohibitive.

Julie waved Hortense from the room. Her vivacious black eyes roved to Ken's face, then to the window. "Go on," she suggested.

"Tell me the rest."

"There's little to tell, Julie. Just remain calm, will you? No storms, please. It's an open-and-shut business matter. Due to your great beauty and consummate artistry, the play is doing capacity business. The instant your understudy took over we'd suffer at the box-office. People would properly feel there is just one Julie Trotter and —"

"Ken, flattery won't work."

"No flattery intended," he said with a nice show of earnestness. "I'm merely stating facts. If you can successfully dispute the facts, I'll be the first to cheer. Why will I be the first to cheer? Because then I'd be near you all summer. Shall I continue?"

Julie compressed her lips. At twenty-nine she was a striking woman close to her physical prime. She had one of those rare, perfectly symmetrical faces that managed to combine a certain inner strength with its outer expression of delightful feminine softness. Her normal complexion was rosy. The normal tendency of her wide-spaced eyes was to sparkle. And this rosiness and this sparkle had a magnetic quality that drew you to her like a steel filing. Julie Trotter knew this, just as she knew that her good figure and carriage had their allures as well, and it was natural for her to take advantage of the fact that she was deemed lovely.

"I'd like you to be near me all summer," she confided, her voice soft. "I think I'd like that very much."

Well, Ken thought, here we go again. The whole thing bothered him. When would Julie be her age? When would she overcome that childish desire to play?

"The facts are," he continued carefully, "that we can't risk permitting Sylvia to play the part without supervision. And Frank can't be in two places at the same time."

"But Sylvia's wonderful in the part, darling."

"Sylvia plods. You know it, I know it. She's a good dramatic actress, but she just can't handle comedy."

"How ridiculous!"

Ken saw no point in prolonging it. "Anyway," he said, "that's the decision, Julie."

She sat up. Now the black eyes blazed. "You might have discussed it with me first."

"There wasn't time. Things are moving swiftly up there in Saunder's Bluff. The hotel is giving us a favorable rate for the troupe — something we didn't expect. And furthermore —"

"I'm entitled to rest! Am I a machine? Even machines are rested from time to time. You ought to be ashamed!"

Now the rain thickened on the windows of the cool, spacious living-room. The rain turned the window-panes opaque. The rain filled the room with a soft drumming sound.

Julie sprang to her feet. Her bosom heaved, her hands rose gracefully to toy agitatedly with the belt of her hostess gown. She said hoarsely: "Tell me the real reason, Ken. Tell me you don't love me, that it's all been an illusion. Why not tell me the real truth?"

"Julie, you know better."

She pounced!

"I'm not blind! I'm not deaf! I saw you with that impossible blonde the other day. Do you think I'm blind?"

Ken swallowed hard. Blast it, was Julie everywhere? Why couldn't a fellow take a girl out, when the mood struck him, without wondering if Julie would see them?

"Ha! You don't answer, sir! And your expression! If that isn't convincing proof of your guilt, I'd like to know what would be."

"It was business," Ken said lamely. "I'm thinking of putting on a new play this October. I don't know if that girl will be good in the spot I have to fill, but —"

"The answer is no, Mr. Albright. I refuse. I'm entitled to my vacation and I intend to have my vacation. And if you doubt that I can have it, I suggest you re-read my contract."

Ken stood up. A veteran of such scenes, he knew what to do and he did it. "Suit yourself, Julie. If you wish to insist I can't prevent it. But it would mean the end of our association and I would be sorry, very sorry about that. You see, I'd been counting upon you to come up to Saunder's Bluff sometime in August. I thought that together we'd have a fine vacation. Still —"

"No. Absolutely not!"

Good grief, Ken wondered, why had he gotten into this profession? There'd been other professions open to a man with capital and a certain willingness to take risks.

"Either I take the summer off, Mr. Albright, or we're finished."

"As you wish."

Good strategy dictated a quick departure, and Ken strode out to the hall for his hat. He picked the hat from the refectory table and continued to the front door. When he opened the front door a damp, cool breeze blew in. It refreshed him, and he laughed. "Ever go walking in the rain, Julie?"

"Ken, we'd drown!"

"I intend, Julie, to walk all the way down to the Battery. I think it would be fun. It's a long time since we had fun, Julie, isn't it?"

She said bitterly: "You use me, Ken. You take advantage of my devotion. You use me as you use everyone else."

Big Ken Albright turned. His blue eyes were narrowed, his chin was truculent. "If you ever say that again, Julie, I'll fire you."

She bit her lip.

"What fine devotion you show, Julie. Here I am up to my neck in a difficult business problem, and you throw temperament at me. Bah. I'll take my walk alone, and you're free to do whatever you darned well please."

There was a long, long silence, and all Ken's nerves went taut in the suspense of waiting for Julie's answer.

Then she came as he'd been hoping she would, came with a quick rush, came with a soft cry, came with strong and eager arms that went up around his neck, came with warm red lips that found his and held them while tears came welling from her eyes.

"You do love me, Ken, don't you?"

"Julie, dear —"

"Sometimes I hate you! I shouldn't feel this way. It should be the other way, the way it is with other men. You should be begging me for a kiss."

"Julie, dear —"

"Ken, don't go. Have some iced coffee. I'll dress, and then we'll go for a walk in the rain."

"Great. And it doesn't matter that you'll probably catch cold and be unable to perform.

There. That shows I'm not the hard-hearted producer you seem to think I am."

Julie clutched at her throat. "Ken, I can't afford to be ill, you know that!"

"Well, what about dinner tonight?"

"Wonderful, Ken."

Going back uptown a few minutes later, Ken felt proud of himself. He'd only be a few minutes late for lunch. Not bad timing. Sometimes, he thought, he was a genius. Well, there it was. Julie would behave, and now he could concentrate on the project up in Saunder's Bluff. It ought to be, he decided, a very interesting and worthwhile summer. . . .

CHAPTER 6

His reappearance in Saunder's Bluff delighted Laura Staley. Just looking at that handsome face gave her morale a lift. They ought to cage Mr. Ken Albright, she thought, and exhibit him wherever feminine morale was low. How did any man grow to be so handsome? How many billions of years of evolution went into the creation of such male pulchritude? Miss Julie Trotter was certainly a fortunate woman. Imagine being as beautiful and talented as Miss Trotter was, and also being the darling of Mr. Albright!

As the big fellow approached the registration counter, Laura smiled. "Delighted to have you with us again, Mr. Albright. I received your wire, and I've assigned you a pleasant room on the third floor. You wanted singles, didn't you?"

"Singles. Miss Staley, may I present Mr. Abernathy, my architect, and Mr. Jones, my director? Gentlemen, a very kind and helpful lady, Miss Laura Staley."

Mr. Abernathy, short and short of breath, wheezed: "How do you do." Mr. Jones, stocky and rumpled, said: "A real thrill." The gentlemen then registered, and Laura took them upstairs in the elevator to the third floor. Laura was very excited and didn't care if they saw that. Out on the third floor main hall, she gave a sweeping gesture with her arm. "This is where your troupe will be housed, Mr. Albright. I thought that possibly you'd prefer a floor to yourselves, and if there's no objection to doubling up we can just squeeze everyone in."

"Splendid, Miss Staley. Technicians, apprentices and staff included, we should number about twenty-five."

"Of course," Laura said, "I have different plans for Miss Trotter. My father owns a nice cottage farther down Corkscrew Creek. We thought Miss Trotter would like that."

The stocky and rumpled man named Mr. Jones looked very puzzled for an instant.

Ken Albright, however, smiled and nodded. "I'm sure Miss Trotter would like that. Of course, I'm not sure she'll be able to spend the summer here. We haven't worked out the details. But I do know she'll be here in August, and I'll let you know about July a bit later in the month."

"Well," wheezed Mr. Abernathy, "shall we

get to our rooms? Personally, I intended to have a nice cold shower by now."

Laura showed them their rooms. She was afraid that their old-fashioned furniture and country simplicity would leave them dissatisfied, but quite the contrary seemed to be the case. The blue eyes of Ken Albright glowed, and even the director, Mr. Jones, seemed to approve.

"Real period setting," Mr. Jones murmured. "A perfect background, boss."

Humming, Laura went back to the lobby. She found that Mr. Williston had returned from lunch and had taken up his position behind the registration desk. She thought of going out for lunch herself, but decided that could wait, and went to her office at the rear to finish checking the books. She switched on her desk lamp, got her calculating machine within easy reaching distance, and glumly settled down for work.

To her relief, the telephone rang. It was Mr. Bowser of the *Clarion*, and he was excited. "Just read that ad you telephoned in this morning, Laura. What sort of girl were you looking for?"

"Elderly and homely, a tireless worker, a person who'll expect only two dollars a week."

He chuckled. "You better watch out," he advised. "If your Pa hears your unbusinesslike approach you'll get paddled."

"Our business has improved since I took over from our Mr. Williston. According to the figures, we're making fifty cents a week more."

"Congratulations."

"Thanks, Mr. Bowser."

"The reason I asked about the kind of girl you wanted is that I know a woman who can use a job."

Laura stopped joking. "She has a job now, Mr. Bowser."

"Well, don't you think you ought to know something about her?"

"I do know something about her. She needs a job, period. It must be horrible to need work and not be able to find it."

"Well . . ."

"Send her over, Mr. Bowser. Around three would be fine. Incidentally, I have news for you. Mr. Albright's back in town, with his architect, Mr. Jerome Abernathy, and his director, Mr. Frank Jones."

He laughed proudly. "I've already got that in type."

"Huh?"

"Well, he wrote me, Laura. He expects to get to work on Brad's barn right away, and he told me to run an ad for a couple of carpenters and electricians and painters."

"Isn't it exciting?"

"You talked to her honor the Mayor lately?"

There'd been no time, Laura remembered, to talk to anyone lately.

"No," she said, "I've not talked with Mayor Wolfe lately."

"Well, why don't you?"

He hung up then.

Laura grinned. She rang for Mrs. Brigham, and when Mrs. Brigham appeared she gestured at the books. "I've decided," she announced, "that you do these better than I ever will, Mrs. Brigham. So I'm turning them over to you."

"Laura. I have enough work."

"Naturally, for more work you should be paid more money. Say twenty dollars a month more?"

Mrs. Brigham chuckled. "How long do you expect to last around here, Laura? Not that it's any of my business, but you should always haggle. That's the proper business way."

But Laura was at the oval wall-mirror, tidying her hair. "I'll be back around four, Mrs. Brigham. Incidentally, Mr. Albright and his party are to have special service. Anything within reason, that is."

"Certainly."

"And while I'm out, Mrs. Brigham, will you delicately convey to Mr. Williston that sulking won't help him a bit? The fact is he wasn't doing a proper job of managing this hotel, that Dad would have demoted him in any case. I don't want to rebuke him myself. Still . . ."

"He's leaving at the end of the month."

"Oh?"

Mrs. Brigham shrugged. "What did your father expect?"

It troubled Laura. Walking to Town Hall at the farther side of the Common, she was deeply troubled by the thought that the resignation had actually been forced by herself that day she'd visited her father's headquarters in Vermont Court to tell him she'd decided to enter his business. It was all well and good for her father to have claimed that Mr. Williston had been unsatisfactory all along. The fact remained that until she'd agreed to enter the business her father had exhibited no displeasure or dissatisfaction with Mr. Williston. That being the case, wasn't this really the old story of a person who needed a job being forced out of a job by a person who certainly didn't need one?

She shivered in the warm, late May air. About halfway across the Common she had the impulse to go back to the hotel to have a long chat with Mr. Williston. But the sight of Mayor Rachel Wolfe coming down the white steps of Town Hall drove the impulse from her mind. She lengthened her stride to intersect the Mayor's progress over near the ornamental pool and bubbling, spraying fountain. One thing at a time, she decided, and the Mayor's attitude toward the Albright Players *was* important.

"Hi," she said. "And how are civic affairs, Mrs. Wolfe?"

"Now there's a fine, subtle approach. You must have inherited your skill from your father."

"I've known for years that I'm rather obvious. I strive to improve. Invariably, I fail."

Mrs. Wolfe glanced about and chose a satisfactory bench in a deep pool of shade. She sat down, crossed her thick legs awkwardly, as usual, and gave the usual tug to get the hem of her skirt down over her knees. She was colorful that afternoon in a print acetate dress. Her gray hair had been worked into neat curls and waves. Her nail polish had been applied properly, for a change, as had her lipstick. Studying her, Laura decided that the Mayor was headed for some social or study group, to make a speech.

"Busy, Mrs. Wolfe?"

The hazel eyes turned hard. "What favor am I in a position to do for you, Laura?"

"None, really. It's merely that I've heard rumors you're opposed to the summer theater.

I was curious to know if that's true."

"I am."

Stated firmly, almost belligerently, it put Laura on the defensive.

She said, puzzled: "You of course have reasons that seem good to you."

"I do. To state them briefly, I think that Mr. Albright is a big-city operator trying to do himself some financial good. In itself, that's no crime. We all try to earn money. But it does seem to me that in the course of trying to do himself some good, he'll do this community much harm. So I'm opposed to the whole enterprise."

A robin flitted by, followed by half a dozen more. A lovely sound of warbling filled the afternoon air, and across the green, beautifully trimmed lawn the playing fountain gurgled. Laura thought restlessly that it was too lovely a day for unpleasantness. Rather, it was a day for telephoning Brad, for saddling up horses, for riding off to the hills for a pleasant time outdoors.

"Those are rather serious charges, Mrs. Wolfe, aren't they?"

"Laura, you're not a business person, but you are very bright. Now consider this as I must. There is absolutely no chance for Mr. Albright to make money here. Not this year, at least. He's no fool, believe me. I've had several good talks with him. He knows that he won't make money here, just as I know it. Yet here he is spending good money to lease the barn at an outrageous figure. He's about to spend more good money to transform that barn into a kind of theater. He'll spend even more money to bring twenty-five to thirty persons out here, at full salary, to put on his plays. Why? To make money?"

"Certainly."

"Laura, that barn couldn't hold an audience larger than five hundred — and they'd have to be squeezed in, believe me. He'd have to fill the barn to capacity every weekend, and probably charge two dollars at a minimum, if he hoped to get any kind of return on his investment. Agreed?"

"Glory, I wouldn't know."

"Well, total up the costs and you'll know. And so the obvious thought has occurred to me that Mr. Albright hasn't come here to make money but to lose money."

Laura blinked, startled.

Mayor Rachel Wolfe shrugged her broad shoulders. "Oh, that's often done by businessmen who are making big money. If they operate something at a loss they very often gain a favorable tax position. And Mr. Albright, incidentally, with two smash hit plays on Broadway in New York City, is certainly making big money. You see?"

Laura did see — or thought, at any rate — that the Mayor was taking a great deal for granted. She said as much, studying the little rainbow gleaming in the spray rising so prettily from the fountain.

Mayor Wolfe shrugged again. "Well, perhaps I am taking much for granted. Still, my views make more sense than the views of a great many around here. Laura, do you know what's going on in your home town? Otherwise intelligent and conservative people are suddenly spinning ridiculous daydreams. Every day I receive petitions for permits to build cabins or to renovate houses for the purpose of renting same to tourists. I have on my desk right this minute outright demands that zoning laws be changed so that people who own property in strictly residential areas may rent extra rooms. And the merchants! Why, several are in New York and Boston right this minute to order big supplies of merchandise. They're ordering on memo, incidentally. Why? Because in the view of everyone great times are coming to Saunder's Bluff. There, that's what's happening in your home town."

Her vehemence surprised Laura. "In other words, you expect that Mr. Albright will pull out the instant he's lost the money he wants to lose?"

"I don't expect anything, one way or the other. But I do think Mr. Albright should be committed by contract to operate his theater a certain number of years before he's welcomed so enthusiastically to Saunder's Bluff."

"To protect the town, in other words?"

"I'm elected to do that, aren't I?"

And she'd do it, too, her expression said, regardless of what anyone else in town said about her, regardless of the fact that it might cost her the election next year!

Laura was impressed. There, she thought, was the personification of New England's justifiably famous sense of duty.

She smiled fondly at the woman's chubby face. "You're very nice, Mrs. Wolfe."

"Thank you, Laura. Now if there's nothing else you want to know I'd better get over to the school. I'm to deliver an address on the joys of public service to the high school seniors. Amusing, don't you think?"

Laura laughed softly. "Oh, it isn't as bad as it sounds, you know. By the way, have you noticed that the offending sign is now up on the roof of the hotel? It menaces nothing any more except the birds that like to sit on the roof."

"I have noticed you're not wearing Brad's ring."

Laura flushed. She said nothing, however.

"Have you broken your engagement to Brad?"

"No."

"Well, then . . ."

"It just seemed silly to continue wearing it, that's all. Brad's a bit annoyed. He actually accused me the other day of trying to pressure him into a hasty and ill-advised act. I wouldn't do that, now would I?"

Her face, so young, her color, so traitorous, made Mrs. Wolfe sharply uneasy. "Speaking as a politician, Laura, I think I ought to warn you that pressure is dangerous technique. You exert pressure here, and pressure is exerted elsewhere. And under pressure, sometimes, something breaks. Then what?"

Laura scowled. Why was there so much unpleasantness to think about on such a pleasant spring day?

"I wouldn't know," she answered. "And I really don't care, Mrs. Wolfe."

Yet she did care, and knowing that was unpleasant, too. Why was Brad sulking? He'd smashed their plans, not she. What right did Brad, of all people, have to be so furious?

Thoughtful, disturbed, she waved goodbye to Mayor Wolfe and ambled on back home for her lunch.

CHAPTER 7

The Albright Players didn't arrive in Saunder's Bluff until June 10th. That annoyed Frank Jones, who didn't hesitate to tell Laura so. "I'm a genius bogged down by mediocrity," he lamented. "Remove my feet from the bog of mediocrity and I'd soar." He looked so pained, so downright discouraged, that Laura had to laugh. And that was a mistake. Thus encouraged, Frank Jones stepped briskly into her office at the hotel and calmly took a cane-seated chair. He gazed about with interest, studying the old and faintly yellowed paper on the wall, her old-fashioned rolltop desk, the ancient wooden file cabinet. None of this was done critically, however. "Nice atmosphere," Frank Jones pronounced. "You don't suit the atmosphere, but that's the fault of the casting director. How come a girl like you is in a business like this?"

She said solemnly: "Pop wants another million before he retires. I don't know why; he just does."

Frank Jones crossed his legs. He was the sloppiest-looking man Laura had ever seen. His outfit for the day consisted of gray flannel slacks, a white, long-sleeved shirt with an open collar, a green sleeveless sweater. Each item of his apparel was clearly expensive, but his trousers were spotted and badly wrinkled, his shirt needed laundering, the green sweater needed patching. She marveled that a man could function successfully in a profession that stressed appearance. She also marveled that a man could treat such expensive things so carelessly.

"Something bothering you?" he asked.

She thought a hint might help, and she deliberately took several laundry tally-sheets from her desk. "Did I remember to tell you, Mr. Jones, that laundry and dry-cleaning service is available through us?"

He scratched his head. His hair was rumpled, too; rather lusterless and dry-looking brown hair with flecks of gray scattered through it. "I'll remember," he said. "Of course, I don't use those services very often. I'd just as soon buy a new shirt as I need one."

"You must be a millionaire, too."

A step sounded in the hall and Ken Albright poked his golden head in. He smiled broadly and took the other cane-seated chair near the wall. "Any time he becomes a nuisance, Miss Staley, just throw him out. You have to watch Frank. Frank moves in on you. But otherwise he's a fine fellow."

Laura wondered what they wanted.

She quickly found out.

Ken Albright leaned forward intently. "About Mayor Wolfe," he said. "Does she have the power to close us down before we even open?"

"I beg your pardon."

The blue eyes twinkled, and it occurred to Laura they could be very warm and very engaging eyes. She wondered why Julie Trotter hadn't married him. A fellow like that should never be permitted to run around loose for long.

"There are rumors," he explained, "that Mayor Wolfe doesn't like us."

"Rumors here, as elsewhere, are just rumors, aren't they?"

Frank Jones stood up, still miffed because his players hadn't come on the day scheduled. "You should always ignore rumors," he advised. "Take me. I listened to a rumor that my kids would be here four days ago. I was a dope. I made all sort of plans. But are they here?"

"They'll be here this morning," Ken Albright said. "We ran into a few difficulties."

"I'll believe it when I see it. What I came in here for, Miss Staley, was to take you out to the theater. Brad and I got to talking about plantings that would give the place a real atmosphere, and Brad says you're the person who knows about things like that."

Laura studied the round and red and wrinkled face. It seemed to her that its expression was saying more than Frank's words were. There were mischievous twinkles deep in the man's wash-gray eyes. What was he up to? He'd termed himself a sentimentalist. Was he sentimentally going about the business of trying to patch up her relations with Brad?

"Well, Miss Staley?"

She spoke coolly, evenly. "I'm afraid you've been misinformed, Mr. Jones. Anyway, if the crowd is coming today I'll be very busy."

"Scaredy-cat!"

She blinked.

Ken Albright chuckled. "Do forgive him, Miss Staley. He does have genius, you see."

Frank walked out, his back conveying a strong disapproval that would have been amusing under other circumstances.

As it was, Laura felt annoyed. She felt annoyed with Frank Jones and with Brad Holbrook and with Ken Albright. She felt annoyed with her job at the hotel, and she felt annoyed with the life of dissatisfaction and tension she was living in Saunder's Bluff. She wanted to go to Boston for a vacation with her grandfather on Beacon Hill. The old goat would probably insist that they play golf every day, morning and afternoon rounds at that, but the change would be pleasant for all that.

"He's a nice fellow," Ken Albright said suddenly. "Your fellow Brad Holbrook, I mean. He's quite clever and industrious, isn't he? I imagine that if he had capital behind him he'd go a long way."

The one thing she wouldn't do, Laura decided, was discuss that.

"But if you'd rather not discuss him, we won't. To return to the subject of Mayor Wolfe, Miss Staley. It seems her opposition to us is based upon a theory she has that I'm here only to lose money. Correct?"

He got around, this big fellow! He missed nothing!

"There is some talk of that sort," she told him. "I don't know what the basis for it is, but —"

"Actually, she's in error. First of all, if my purpose were to lose money, I would arrange to lose it more conveniently in New York. I would produce a poor play. When I had sustained the loss I wanted I would close the play. It would be much more simple that way, you see?"

Laura did see, and she was surprised that Mayor Wolfe hadn't thought about that. She grinned broadly. "Why don't you mention that to Mayor Wolfe?"

"If necessary, I shall. I would prefer, however, to have some interested party, such as you, do that. If, of course, the need arises."

"But —"

"Did you get Julie's picture?"

Laura's gray eyes shone. She nodded excitedly. "I'm having it framed — and her note, too. When I'm very old I'll show them both to my grandchildren and —"

"Are you that silly, Miss Staley?"

"I beg your pardon?"

He stood up, frowning now, apparently disturbed. "I mean, who is Julie Trotter? An actress. A very successful and very talented actress. Nothing more. And the world is filled with successful, talented people. You saw one a few minutes ago in the person of Frank Jones. Yet you clearly weren't thrilled by him. Why are people always so thrilled when they meet or see or get a letter from an actress?"

"Oh, it's the glamour, I suppose. It's part of the eternal love of make-believe. Anyway, I was thrilled and I am thrilled and I'm not ashamed to say so, either."

"Julie's really a very stupid woman, Miss Staley. She is likable, and she does have beauty. But the only remarkable thing about Julie is her talent. And it isn't so much a talent for acting as it is a talent for following directions exactly. I think that if Frank worked as hard with you as he has with Julie you'd be quite as successful."

"Oh, sure."

"Ever think in terms of a career on the stage, Miss Staley?"

It was so preposterous Laura threw her glossy black head up and laughed. She was very lovely, and Ken Albright's blue eyes narrowed.

"It really isn't preposterous," he said firmly. "You have uncommon beauty, Miss Staley; you have natural grace. Frank commented about those just this morning."

"But it would be make-believe, don't you see? What would it all amount to? Would it be a home, would it be a baby in a girl's arms? Uh-uh. Even if I were twice as lovely as Miss Trotter, and very, very talented, I'd prefer a home and my children to the theater, believe me."

"Really?"

"And you haven't flattered me into agreeing to talk to Mayor Wolfe for you, Mr. Albright. I hate to put it so bluntly, but my father always says that plain speaking is best."

He laughed. "Oh, was I doing that?"

She met the laughing blue eyes. She surprised something very warm in them, and for some queer reason she tingled. My, she thought, how he could charm even when he seemed disinterested in charming! A simple country girl would have to watch this Mr. Ken Albright.

Her silence, her grave gray eyes, seemed to disconcert him. Abruptly, he stopped laughing. "You're a very strange woman, Miss Staley. You're very difficult to peg."

She glanced at her desk clock. If the Albright Players were due to arrive they would arrive on the eleven o'clock train. It was now ten-thirty. The Players would require transportation from the railroad station, and finding transportation for fifteen or twenty persons wouldn't be easy.

"I'm merely a small-town business girl," she told him, gently, "who thinks that if your people are coming on the morning train they should be met with adequate transportation. My car will seat six and our local cab will seat six more. I'll have to arrange for other cars. Will three more do?"

"One more. I haven't given Frank the bad news yet, but Manny Cohen, my business manager, has cut the troupe down to fifteen. Manny insists that for this first year costs must be kept to a minimum. A couple of technicians will drive up here later in the month. Much of the work can be done by the players who aren't cast in the play being put on, and —"

"Well, I'll have our bookkeeper meet the train, too. Luggage can be picked up later by truck."

She got up and went across the hall to Mrs. Brigham's sunlit, warm, very tiny office. Mrs. Brigham was working industriously despite the heat but was very happy to be dragged away from her calculating-machine. She was just a bit nervous, however, at the prospect of having to drive actors and actresses anywhere. "They're different," she explained. "I'm told that most of them are actually crazy."

"Well, you'll live."

With time a factor Laura hurried back to her office. She dialed Mayor Wolfe's office and gave her the news. Mayor Wolfe, inevitably, was less than enthusiastic but she did concede, speaking purely as a politician, that a show of fair play couldn't possibly do her an injury and might do her a great deal of good. She closed the conversation with a prophecy of doom and a promise to drag Mr. Bowser of the *Clarion* to the station with her for the purpose of publicizing the arrival of the Albright Players. Laura was chuckling by then, and she wagged her head after she'd hung up. "Mayor Wolfe," she predicted, "will be the mayor of Saunder's Bluff until she retires. That woman can think of more angles more quickly than anyone I know."

She paused, struck by a sudden thought.

"Except you, of course, Mr. Albright. Incidentally, why don't you invite her to lunch and talk to her as plainly as you've talked to me? Goodness, this is a small town. Mayor Wolfe's a fine person who isn't carried away by any notion she's terribly important."

"Well, perhaps I will. Incidentally, do you ever accept invitations to lunch? You've been very kind and helpful, Miss Staley. I'd like to express my appreciation."

"What, and give Miss Trotter reason to think she was wrong to write me such a sweet note?"

"I'm not engaged to her, you know."

It stopped Laura short, halfway to the door. Her brow wrinkled. "But I thought I'd read in the papers that you are."

"Publicity arouses interest in a star, Miss Staley, and that interest has a cash value to a producer. You must always be skeptical when you read such publicity."

Laura was shocked, and her face revealed it. "But surely you wouldn't release publicity of that sort just to cash in at the box office?"

"Why not?"

Laura bit her lip. She felt disappointed by him, but she wisely kept it to herself. After all, it was none of her business. She was simply the manager of a country hotel that was making money on the Albright party and would make even more money because of the Albright Players. She must remember that. Business was business.

"We'd better get to the station," she said. "If you like you can ride with me. Since only fifteen are coming there'll be extra room."

He politely stepped aside and allowed her to precede him from the office. He stood quietly by while she issued instructions to Mr. Williston and then, just as quietly, he accompanied her to her Ford in the parking-lot at the rear. It wasn't until they were seated in her car and driving toward the station at the east end of town that he returned to the subject. And then it was merely to say: "Some day, Miss Staley, we must have a long chat on the subject of values. It should be interesting. In the meantime, what about considering my lunch invitation seriously? I'm certain Brad Holbrook wouldn't object."

His tone caught her attention. "Why are you so certain?" she challenged. "Perhaps here in New England we don't take engagements so lightly."

"But I'm the goose, you see, that's laying

the golden egg. Your Brad Holbrook has a strong interest in golden eggs."

Her temper flared. "You're strange, Mr. Albright. You aren't a bit the way I thought you were the first time I saw you. You looked so pleased with James Monroe Street, you were so nice to the children, you seemed so quiet and friendly and peaceful and — but you're not, are you?"

He shrugged. "You know," he said, "truth is truth. And you must always be careful, Miss Staley, not to believe that your own values are the only values to live by. I shocked you, back there in your office. Yet it's an old and accepted practice of the theater to publicize the emotional interests of an important female star. A star very often sells that very thing about Julie Trotter that has impressed you — glamour. A glamorous figure must naturally arouse the interest of many men — if she doesn't then she isn't a glamorous figure. You see? Quite possibly I lent my name to a device that would be of help to Julie. Quite possibly I never approved. You really don't know, do you?"

"Well —"

"And I really wasn't endeavoring to seem a worldly, jaded cynic when I mentioned the goose and the golden egg. I was stating a fact. Possibly I was even endeavoring to be kind.

You really don't know, do you?"

"I —"

Again, he interrupted. And now his deep voice had a pleasant warmth, and there was peace in it too.

"You don't wear his ring now, Miss Staley. Why not? To signify your displeasure? To impress upon him the fact that you won't wait forever? Or perhaps to convey to the men of this region that you're available again, should any of them be interested in dating you?"

Laura's cheeks burned. "That's ridiculous!"

"Merely one interpretation, Miss Staley. But if I had interpreted your action that way, and if I had invited you to lunch merely to help you with your very unoriginal attempt to apply pressure to Brad Holbrook — well, why should you be so angry with me?"

Laura looked grimly at the road.

"Of course," he said, "I had no intention of offending you, Miss Staley. Why should I offend you? You have been very kind, and I am appreciative."

"Do others think that way?"

"I'm afraid so. I know that Holbrook does, that Frank Jones does. Ah — that's the whistle, isn't it?"

It was, and Laura had never welcomed the raucous hooting of the *Corsair*'s whistle more than she did right then. She felt so ashamed of herself she wanted to crawl into a hole somewhere and pull the hole in after her. Glory, if she were being *that* obvious Brad was doubtless laughing at her. And Ken Albright, too? She gave his face a sidelong glance.

He surprised her. "No," he said, "I never laugh at troubled people. I like people too well, you see."

CHAPTER 8

The *Corsair* came in with a fine snorting and clanging and grinding commotion that brought kids running from all directions. Black smoke billowed skyward, the engineer waved a gloved hand in cheery fashion at one and all, and then the locomotive surged past the yellow station-house and the train hissed and jolted to a halt. A small, very peppy redhead was the first passenger to detrain. She gave a quick glance in all directions, then whooped: "Hey, we've reached the sticks!" Now others came rushing down the car steps to the platform, all of them young, all of them excited, all of them filling the air with gay chatter. It was the redhead who spotted Ken Albright. The redhead charged over, a pert, sassy thing in slacks who apparently never permitted rank to inhibit her. She threw her arms around Ken's neck. "Boss," she said, "I love you. We're having a heat wave in New York. In another two days all I'd have been —"

She smiled politely at Laura. "How do you do," she said. "If you're in love with Mr. Albright, don't mind me, because everyone knows I'm silly."

"Sally Ewing," Ken Albright explained, "is one of my more talented people, Miss Staley. Sally, mind your manners."

Others came over, and Ken Albright introduced them as they came, but they were just a blur of faces to Laura and she didn't bother to try to attach names to any of them. She just led them all over to Mayor Wolfe, who was standing somewhat grimly near the station-house, and introduced them to the Mayor as the Albright Players. Mr. Bowser signaled to a photographer, who took a flashlight picture. Then Mayor Wolfe made a gracious speech of welcome, and Ken Albright made one in turn. It was all smoothly and expertly done, and then the little crowd broke up and bedlam ensued. Inevitably, there was an incident. A small fellow who seemed to fancy himself in the role of a devil-may-care fellow walked over to a nearby horse and yelled: "Boo!" The horse reared. The horse flattened its ears alongside its head and made a move toward the small fellow. "Help!" he bellowed. "It's alive!" Laura got between him and the horse and laughingly stroked the menacing head. "Be a big boy, will you?" she asked the fellow. "This poor creature's ready to be retired."

"Aren't you afraid?"

His eyes went up and down, then sparkled.

"My name," he announced, "is Ronnie Case. Of course, I'm the star of this organization. Now if you'll just give me your telephone number, you dear thing, I'll —"

"Nix."

Hugely annoyed, Ronnie Case turned to meet Sally Ewing's bright green eyes. "Nix?"

"Nix. According to the boss, everyone has to behave. Don't tell me what your idea of good behavior is, because it doesn't count. All I know is that the boss said the ladies of Saunder's Bluff are really ladies."

"How dull!"

The pert redhead now jerked a thumb over her left shoulder. At this point Ronnie Case flushed, but it was significant that he did go back to the crowd milling about on the station platform. Sally Ewing, quite nonchalant, linked her arm around Laura's. "You'll like Ronnie," she said. "Actually, he's just a kid. I understand I'm to ride with you."

"Fine. Incidentally, though, I didn't need to be rescued."

"Ronnie did."

"Oh?"

"The boss likes you, Miss Staley. You can

always tell. When the boss likes a girl he develops a fine protective attitude. You'll notice it yourself. Well, to make it short, Ronnie has a lot of ability and he could go far under Mr. Albright. Catch?"

Rattled, Laura looked at big Ken Albright. He was bustling about, getting his actors and actresses into the cars. He seemed less their employer than just another good-looking fellow trying to make good in the theater. He laughed at this one, teased that one, playfully rumpled a stunning blonde's hair.

The redhead was annoyed. "That blonde," she said, "is Pru Drake. If you have a boy friend, Miss Staley, watch Pru. Do you know anything about the history of the Vikings?"

"Well . . ."

"Well, that athletic-looking hunk of blonde is just like the Vikings of old. She hits and runs. In other words, she raids. Or, to put it another way, whatever you have she wants, period."

Laura gave the redhead a searching glance. "You sound very bitter, Miss Ewing."

"Oh, call me Sally. Sure I'm bitter. Do you see that lean and handsome guy who looks like Hamlet brooding on a wall? Well, that guy happens to be John Grover, one of our romantic leads. And he happened to be mine until the Viking hit and ran. Now all he does is brood. Why, I hope to tell you I'm bitter!"

But, it developed, still hopeful. Laura didn't quite see how the sassy redhead accomplished it, but when she drove her quota of the Albright Players back to the hotel the redhead and brooding Hamlet were beside her on the front seat. The fact that Hamlet continued to brood didn't seem to discourage Miss Sally Ewing a jot. She chattered throughout the ride to the hotel, and later, in the lobby, she stuck to her Johnny like glue.

And that, curiously, was the memory Laura took home with her at the end of the long, tiring day. Under the shower she wondered if perhaps she shouldn't borrow a leaf from Sally Ewing's book and do some plain and determined "sticking" to Brad. Perhaps in the long run that was the only technique that would work. Perhaps her present technique was actually hurting her, rather than helping her? She thought about it through a lonely dinner in the dining-room. She thought about it the next day as well. And then, on an impulse, she got into her car at the lunch hour and drove through the drizzling rain out to the Holbrook farm. She caught Brad striding off across his yard toward the barn. He was a tense and tired figure in his dirty jeans and rubberized raincoat, and his first reaction to the visit was a quick tightening of his lips.

That startled her.

"Hi, Brad."

"Hi, Laura."

"Long time no see, Brad. And it's just occurred to me that since tonight is Mrs. Bennett's night off, you might like to try some of my cooking."

He scratched his lean, unshaven face. His brown eyes met hers briefly, then flicked away. "I don't know, Laura. It isn't much fun to sit at table with a fellow who's against you."

"I meant here, Brad. Brad, it would be such fun. And then after dinner you could show me through the barn. I haven't had time to see the changes, you know."

"Look, are you saying you're sorry?"

"Brad, I —"

"Because I'll tell you something, Laura. When I say I'll marry a girl, I will. And when I say I love a girl, I do. And I like to be believed, and I like to be trusted. And here's something else. I'm tired. I'm tired of working so hard. It isn't fun. But more than that, I'm tired of being engaged but not engaged. That hurts. So if you're saying you're sorry and you're wearing the ring, okay. But if you're just trying to kill some time and you're not wearing the ring, that's different."

"I see."

He turned to glower down at her frankly. "You might as well know the rest. I been thinking. I been thinking about you and me, about the chances I have, about your father, about a lot of things. And I'll give it to you straight, Laura. The duty of a breadwinner is to bring in money. That's his first duty, and I'll do my duty. And so I've been thinking that the earliest we can get married is next June. The thousand dollars I'm getting for the barn this year has made things kinda different."

"Obviously, Brad."

"Will you stop using that tone?"

Laura turned and walked back to her car. She thought that if she just could get into her car and drive away without speaking another word things would be all right. Hearing him squishing after her through the mud and the thickening rain, she broke into a run. But he could run faster than she could, and did. He reached the Ford before she did, and efficiently blocked off the door.

"Let's say it all!" he shouted. "Let's get it settled once and for all."

"Brad, get out of my way, please."

"I'm a louse. That's it, isn't it? I'm just a grubbing earthworm whose thoughts and ideas don't count, isn't that it?"

His face was beet-red now, his brown eyes

bulging and flashing.

"Go on!" he yelled. "Say it!"

"Brad, please let me into the car. I'm being wet."

"Well, my wife don't go hungry. My mother did. You never knew that, did you? Why do you think she's sick so much; why do you think my folks went to California? Because she went hungry, because she's been sick ever since, that's why."

"Brad, I haven't thought any of those horrid things. You know it. You're trying to blame me for your own guilty conscience, and you know that, too."

It seemed to reach his angry mind. His mouth fell agape, and Laura thought for an instant that the ugly scene would end there.

And then his eyes, those hot brown eyes, looked at her hands. The absence of his engagement ring did it.

"Put it back on," he snapped, "or give it to me. If you're my woman you'll trust me and do what I say. If you're not, let's stop fooling around."

"Brad, be your age. You know as well as I do that it can't be like that. It's a partnership. Now stop talking nonsense."

"Either I'm engaged, or I'm not."

"Engaged to do what, Brad?"

"To get married next year, if it's practical."

"And I'm supposed to wait until you decide if it is or isn't practical?"

"Other women wait."

"On those terms?"

"On any terms."

"Brad, are you serious?"

"What it amounts to is that you either do or don't trust me. I won't be laughed at in town."

Laura bit her lip. Now, for the first time, her own temper gave her trouble. But she managed to control herself. She asked tautly but very quietly; "Do you realize, Brad, that if I return it now, after all this, I won't ever wear it again?"

"Meaning you don't love me enough to wait?"

"Meaning I won't be treated as a conscience, Brad."

"Sure, that's right. You're a Staley. We have our pride, we Staleys."

And there it was!

"I see, Brad. That's been the rub all along. I'm a Staley, and you resent the Staleys because one of them doesn't approve of you. That's it, isn't it?"

"All I'm saying is that if you don't want to wear that ring just give it back."

Laura didn't hesitate. She reached into her pocket and stripped the tissue paper from it and gave it a flip in his direction. It was all done so swiftly he never did have a chance to catch it. It disappeared with a splash into a mud puddle.

And now he did startle her. He gasped: "You're returning it?"

"Good luck, Brad. I hope you make your million. I think you will, if that's any consolation. People generally get what they want, and you seem to want money very intensely."

"Listen, Laura —"

Laura didn't, sure that if she did she'd stand there like a fool herself and shout a great many things she didn't want to shout. She pushed by him and wrenched the Ford door open. She got into the car and slammed the door shut. At that moment he seemed to realize she was in deadly earnest, and he gave a queer shout and made a lunge at the car door. But she started the motor anyway, and then she started the car. The next thing that happened was unfortunate. The car's surge forward came so quickly he never did have the time to release the door handle. He was jerked forward and thrown, was Brad Holbrook, and he landed on his hands and knees in the same mud puddle where his ring had landed.

Tears in her eyes, Laura drove on.

CHAPTER 9

Within a week everyone for miles around was intensely aware of the fact that the Albright Players had arrived in Vermont for the summer. Placards announced it, radio advertisements blared it, newspaper stories emphasized it, and Sally Ewing, John Grover, Ronnie Case and Helene Otis bought a jalopy roadster for a "song," or so they thought, and seemed to make it their business to take the jalopy, themselves and their handout publicity folders to every hamlet within an easy day's drive. Because the players were so young and so thrilled to be in the honest-to-goodness country, the countryside made them welcome. There was a great party in Town Hall. There was a great dance in Town Hall. No less a personage than Robert Staley threw a great picnic for them, and not to be outdone, people over near the seacoast gave them a genuine New England clambake. All this was interesting to Mayor Rachel Wolfe. She termed it an eye-opener in the course of a chat she was having with the bank president, Mr. King. "I should learn to watch more and to keep my tongue still," she told him. "This is an eye-opener. This proves conclusively that despite the reputation they enjoy for shrewdness, New Englanders are suckers, too."

"What's that?"

"You heard me. Such a bother! And for what? For a mob of youngsters who probably can't act worth a darn."

Mr. King was vexed, inasmuch as he'd committed his bank to the purchase of a sizable block of season tickets. He said with asperity, "You talk like a sore-head, Rachel. And you haven't learned, it seems, to keep your eyes open and your tongue still."

"And you talk like a banker who has just received a handsome deposit of Albright money."

"Which I have," Mr. King said comfortably. "A remarkable young man, this Kenneth Albright. Without violating a confidence, I think I may tell you the deposit was in five figures."

Mayor Wolfe stirred uneasily.

Mr. King drummed his stubby fingers on his desk. He surveyed the short, thick-set woman who had been elected to high office three times despite his strong opposition. "You must never make the mistake, Rachel, of substituting hunches for facts. I say that until there is concrete evidence to the contrary, Mr. Albright's word should be accepted as trustworthy. Fair play!"

Mayor Wolfe gazed out the arched window that commanded a perfect view of Thomas Jefferson Avenue. A group of the young actresses and actors were strolling along under the elderly maples. All the girls were in slacks and blouses, all the men in shorts and T-shirts. This reversal of the natural order of things irritated the Mayor. "I dislike knobby knees and hairy legs, Mr. King, don't you?"

"Please, Rachel, let's have no such talk here."

Her hazel eyes twinkled. "You're very stuffy, Mr. King. I'll tell you something. The day you announce you feel my candidacy deserves your support is the day I'll retire from politics."

"May I depend on it?"

"Why do you hate me, Mr. King?"

"Not you, Rachel. Fair play! To put it simply and delicately, I feel the place of a woman is in her home. Natural order of things, you know."

"How would I live, Mr. King?"

He had difficulty breathing, suddenly. He coughed and he sneezed. He had to hasten to the water-cooler for a paper cup of iced water. He quaffed this in two gulps, but the cure of his respiratory difficulty wasn't total. He didn't speak, he wheezed. He wheezed: "Do I or do I not stand prepared at all times, Rachel, to offer you my hand? Honesty and fair play, Rachel!"

"If you weren't such a hide-bound conservative!"

He wagged a stubby forefinger gleefully. "Conservative! This from you? A paradox! I am prepared to take the word of a man freely given. You, however, will be content with nothing but outright guarantees. And you dare call me a conservative?"

"That's different. This isn't a personal thing. As the Mayor of Saunder's Bluff, I have a duty to protect the interests of the community."

"Well, if you will take the advice of an experienced man with a reputation for sagacity you'll look him up. You'll find his reputation is sterling. I have already done that."

"Where did he get the money to produce plays?"

"Old Mid-western family. Great holdings in wheat, in lumber, in coal. There's an older brother who manages all that. A genius. So you see, the young man has the resources, and in his background is a wise and knowing brother who won't let him wander off course."

Mayor Wolfe gasped.

"What's that, Rachel?"

"Please don't glance out the window, Mr. King. I am now prepared to agree young ladies should wear slacks and that young men should wear shorts."

However, he did gaze out the window at the tall blonde girl with the broad shoulders, the tawny skin, the beautifully modeled legs.

"How delightful," he said. "It's kind of nature, Rachel, to continue its happy practice of manufacturing those. Who is she?"

"Prudence Drake. Don't let that air of sweet and gentle innocence fool you, however. There's a tigress on the prowl."

He chuckled, did Mr. King, and he looked again.

The cynosure of all eyes, and pleasantly aware that she was, Miss Prudence Drake sauntered on. It was always possible, she thought, that there was some old gink around who would think she was twenty-three skiddoo beautiful and agree to star her in some play. It stood to reason!

Pru stopped short. She tried Smile 3 on the brooding Hamlet who was staring pensively at her ankles. She coughed to make him look up, and she tried Smile 3 again.

"I beg your pardon?" he asked.

"John, there's the dearest millpond over at

other end of town. I just love to swim in a millpond."

"They have frogs," he said. "And you're disobeying orders."

Pru fluttered her golden lashes. "Oh, may I have an arsenic, too?"

Inevitably, the others noticed her and came over led by Sally Ewing, of course. Some day, Pru Drake daydreamed, she'd leave Sally high and dry in the spotlight, like a flopping fish. "Sweet Sally," she cooed, "I know I'm disobeying orders and I'm so terribly, terribly ashamed. But may I point out that I *do* have a figure worth displaying?"

"Pru, do you want to spoil things? Look. Folks in a town like this have different ideas from ours. They don't like half-naked people, for instance, wandering around town. And if you get them snorting what happens to the project?"

"I'm sure I have sufficient talent to go it alone, dear. Naturally, I'm not so sure about you."

Sally flushed. "In just one more minute, Amazon though you are, I'm going to slap your sassy face."

John Grover interrupted. "Let's go swimming," John Grover said. "All of us."

But it wasn't to be. Ronnie Case came driving by in the jalopy. "Big meeting at the barn," he called. "Hop aboard."

By a curious coincidence there wasn't quite room for Pru.

"Tough," said Ronnie. "Real tough."

"For a man who's playing up to Sally while poor John is brooding, you're very bold, aren't you?"

Pru Drake sauntered on, enormously pleased with herself.

She turned left into Franklin D. Roosevelt Avenue. A boy came out of a yard, riding a broomstick pony. "Hi Yi!" the boy screeched. "A hussy! Bang, you're dead!"

"Such a sweet little boy. Tell me, is this the way to Mr. Staley's house?"

The cowpoke now became an Indian. "Ugh," he said.

Pru refused to become rattled. She gave the boy Smile 6. Lest anyone within earshot should misunderstand, she drawled: "I do wish that I had a little boy like you. How sweet. How terribly, terribly sweet."

It worked.

An attractive woman in her middle thirties got up from her knees in the yard. She came over to the picket fence, smiling as mothers will when their ghastly contributions to the race have won compliments. "Is he bothering you, miss? Mike, come ride Silver back into the yard."

"Ugh."

"Such a lovely street," Pru said. "You know, all my life I've read about New England, how it was the cradle of our liberty, how the greatness of America sprang from it, how its brave men sailed forth to the far places of the globe. But I never saw it until this summer. And do you know something? It's lovelier than I thought it was."

"We love it, too."

"These are black walnut trees, aren't they?"

The woman laughed. "My, one can tell you've never been to New England. Those are elms, miss — oh, forgive me; I'm Mrs. Enslen."

"I'm Prudence Drake. I'm with the Albright Players."

"I rather imagined so. Oh, you must let me give you some tea. My grandmother's very excited about the Albright Players. She's almost ninety, but she's determined to see one of your plays. You're opening July 1st, aren't you?"

"So I understand." Pru followed her up the neat brick walk to the three-story, white-frame house. "Of course," she laughed, "with Mr. Albright running things anything is possible. If he isn't pleased with the final appearance of the theater he's likely to postpone the opening until August."

Mrs. Enslen opened the front door. She gestured Pru in, and Pru entered with alacrity. "My, what a dear place, Mrs. Enslen. I do love the quaint, don't you?"

Mrs. Enslen showed her into a large living-room. The shades were three quarters drawn, so that the room was cool and deeply shadowed. But there was enough light for Pru to see that the massive furniture was very old and had been very expensive. "I begin to understand now why Mr. Albright spends so much of his time in the Staley home. He does love lovely old things," she cooed.

"But surely you must be mistaken, Miss Drake! The Staleys prefer modern furniture."

"Really? Why, I thought the attraction there was —"

"Well, there's my grandmother, Miss Drake. Grandmother, this is Miss Drake, one of the stars of the Albright Players."

Dark within dark stirred and rustled over near the fireplace. Pru was startled. But the word "star" rang and echoed through her mind like a beautiful bell, and she controlled the sudden fright that stirring had given her. She advanced regally, her bare legs and arms faintly luminous in the deep shadows. "Delighted, Mrs. Enslen, simply delighted."

"Young lady?"

"Mrs. Enslen?"

"You're a hussy."

Pru smiled. That was a matter of opinion, she thought.

"Naked as a jaybird!"

The younger Mrs. Enslen behind Pru made little sounds of embarrassment. This amused Pru, but she sat down with a little display of embarrassment herself. "I'm sorry you feel as you do, dear Mrs. Enslen. I'm from the South, myself. And in the South it's quite proper for ladies to appear in public in shorts."

A doorbell chimed somewhere, and Pru sat stiffly with the mumbling old hag while Mrs. Enslen went out to answer it.

The caller was the strange young man who owned the barn out on that cute little farm beyond town.

"Brad," Mrs. Enslen the younger said, "you must go in and chat with Grandmother. You can help me plant that bush later. Oh, and will you have some tea or coffee? We're entertaining one of the Albright Players. Miss Prudence Drake."

Pru rose. She glanced about, looking for a good background, and decided the fireplace itself would do, inasmuch as her figure would be sharply limned against its dark brick and stone. She hastened to it, and turned with a pretty cry of pleasure as Mrs. Enslen returned with Mr. Brad Holbrook tagging along beside her.

"Why, it's Mr. Holbrook, Hi, Mr. Holbrook. Mrs. Enslen invited me in to meet her grandmother. Wasn't that kind of her?"

Mrs. Enslen the older mumbled: "Got to watch her, Brad. Naked as a jaybird. A hussy."

"Hello, Grammy."

"Brad, I hear you're not engaged."

Across the room Mrs. Enslen the younger was running up the shades. Now a pleasant golden light came into the old room, and Pru saw the lean face tighten as with pain and felt warmly gleeful.

"Well, Grammy, things happen. You wish they didn't, but they do. Look, Mrs. Enslen, I better get that bush planted."

Pru clapped her hands excitedly. "Oh, may I help? Why, I've never planted a flower, let alone a great big bush."

Mrs. Enslen the younger was touched. "Why, fancy never having planted anything! Why, it seems fantastic. Of course, Miss Drake. Brad will show you the way. And while you're doing that I'll prepare refreshments."

Pru hurried to the living-room door and stood waiting for Brad to show her the way. She was an enchanting sight in her T-shirt and bright red shorts and matching canvas shoes. Brad Holbrook looked at her and flushed. Then, slowly, heavily, he swung out ahead of her and led her out into the large back yard.

"You shouldn't be here," he snapped.

"A mere coincidence, Mr. Holbrook."

"We're not fools up here, even if we are hicks to you. You've been playing up to me ever since you came. Why?"

"La, such conceit!"

"How did you know I'd be here?"

"I heard you say so."

Brad stiffened. "Then you admit it?"

"Why not? I love the truth, Mr. Holbrook. And if the truth is that your handsome face fascinates me, what harm does it do for me to say so?"

He spun. His brown eyes were hot, contemptuous. "You fall pretty quick, Miss Pru Drake."

She was unabashed. "It's been a weakness of mine since babyhood."

"Well, you're in the wrong neck of the woods. And I'm the wrong fellow. I have a girl."

"So does Ken Albright, eh?"

It cut.

He turned to glower at the bush he'd brought along. "Well, we better get this planted."

"She's a fool, Mr. Holbrook. Miss Staley, I mean. I don't think she could ever do better than you."

"What are you up to, will you tell me that?"

Beautiful Pru rolled her lovely eyes. No, she decided, she would not tell him that. It was really much too soon.

"I should think," she said, "that you'd be helping at the barn."

"It's finished. It don't look like a theater to me, but Albright's satisfied. And speaking of the barn — you're in hot water. There was a rehearsal scheduled for this afternoon."

Pru winced. "But I thought —"

"Mr. Jones made a sudden decision. But I guess it doesn't matter, does it?"

Pru whirled. "With Helene Otis making the big play for all the fat parts? Don't be a dunce. You get me out there in a hurry."

Brad just laughed. "I really wish I could," he said. "But you're just beginning to fascinate me. Too bad."

CHAPTER 10

It seemed to Laura that when Pru Drake did finally appear at the rehearsal the beautiful, statuesque blonde was in something of a temper. It also seemed to her that the blonde was considerably annoyed with Miss Laura Staley, of all people. That puzzled Laura, because she couldn't recall having said more than a dozen words to her since the Albright Players had arrived in Saunder's Bluff. Laura's curiosity got the better of her. Bored with the technical proceedings in progress on the stage, she walked down the center aisle of the barn-theater and dropped onto the bench directly behind the actress.

"Dislike your room, Miss Drake?"

"I beg your pardon."

"You gave me such a dirty glance as you went by. If your room's unsatisfactory I'm sure I could change it."

"It's quite a nice room, as rooms go. And I'm sure you must have been mistaken, Miss Staley. True, I was annoyed as I came in. But not with you. With Mr. Jones. Mr. Jones neglected to inform me he contemplated holding a rehearsal today."

"I believe it's a try-out, not a rehearsal, Miss Drake. Now there's a mystery. Since you're all professional actors and actresses, why do you have to try out for parts? Surely professionals can handle any part they're given."

"Some can, some can't. And naturally a person can do one thing better than another. I'm more convincing, for instance, in straight drama than I am in slapstick comedy."

"Rubbish."

Up on the stage Frank Jones bawled: "Take fifteen."

The stage emptied quickly. Laughing, shouting, the fellows and girls hustled outdoors with all the eagerness of kids dashing out for recess. Frank Jones, however, just came down into the auditorium and joined Pru on her bench. Frank was perspiring and breathing hard. His slacks and shirt looked as if they'd just been run through a mangle while damp. "Nice to see you, Amazon," he told Pru. "A real thrill."

"Frank, I wasn't told. I didn't know until I got the news from Mr. Holbrook over at the Enslens'."

Laura wondered what on earth the girl had been doing at the Enslens'. In that costume, of all things! What had Grammy said?

"Oh, it don't make any difference," Frank assured her. "Amazon, our first offering will be that refugee piece. Not to spoil you, but who else could take the lead, huh?"

Pru revealed a new layer of her personality. She wasn't triumphant. Rather, she was just interested and troubled. "You'll have to work with me, Frank. I don't handle that death scene well. I'm too active. Blast it, I huff and puff. That's no way for an actress to act. Why, Helen Hayes or Judith Anderson could convey grief and shock and horror with just one single quirk of an eyebrow."

Frank nodded.

Interested, Laura folded her hands on her lap and frankly eavesdropped.

"What you do wrong," Frank explained very gently, as a father might to a daughter, "is think in terms of acting rather than in terms of emotion. You have to forget that you're acting. You have to be a half-starved Jewish girl crouching beside this cot, watching your mother die. Look. Your whole world has gone to smash. You were a respected teacher, and a beloved teacher, too. Your mother was a fine psychologist, who had the respect and love of the village. Then Hitler came. One day you were suddenly surrounded by fifty or sixty kids of the Hitler Youth organization, and those kids began to hit at you with their leather belts. And they were singing, 'When Jewish blood is drawn by our knives then we'll be happy.' You see? All the world has gone insane, and now there you are, remembering all that while your mother is moaning and dying."

Laura shivered.

Pru laughed.

The laugh jarred.

And then, there in that quiet barn, there occurred something that drew all of Laura's nerves taut and made her scalp tingle. Eerily, frighteningly, that laughter rose to a shrill note of hysteria. But it just touched hysteria, barely suggested it, before it sank to a barely audible sob. And then Pru Drake was out in the aisle, crouching in the aisle, and she *was* a poor creature watching her mother die. The illusion was so powerful Laura could scarcely breathe. The girl's blue eyes were half glazed by hysteria, horror. Her lips were slack, partly open, and with every breath she drew she made a hoarse and pathetic sound of sheer helplessness. An Amazon saucy in shorts and a T-shirt? See how shrunken she was, how sick and confused and frightened and heart-broken she was!

Frank stirred and grunted, and broke the spell.

"Like that?" Pru Drake asked. She came

bounding to her feet, all vigor and beauty again. "Frank, did I —"

She noticed Laura's face, and broke off.

"My gosh," she said, "will you look at the hick?"

At that point Laura wanted to club her.

She said flatly, however: "That was one of the finest things I've seen in years, Miss Drake. Why, I could scarcely believe you were you."

"Maybe," said Frank, "there was too much huffing and puffing. I liked the laugh. Only don't take so long building up to hysteria. Try just a couple of shrill notes. Sock it up to high D say, right at once. That'll startle. You startle 'em and you lift 'em out of the idea you're just acting. Then you have 'em. Oh, and not so many ups and downs of your breathing apparatus. But we'll work it out. I tell you what, kid. You come here tonight for an hour or so. We'll take that scene bit by bit, line by line. Okay?"

"Yes, sir."

Frank chuckled and turned to Laura. "You hear that sir? Until they're stars they call me sir. When they are stars they try to tell *me* what is or isn't acting. It's real funny."

"I'll be different," Pru announced. A likable sincerity rang in her voice. "Whatever I become, Frank, I'll owe to you. I may cut a few corners here and there, but when it comes to work I'm honest, and when someone's good I can honestly admire him."

"A real thrill," said Frank sarcastically. But he was touched, and Laura was amused to notice how correctly Ken had pegged his director.

The other actors and actresses returned. Frank got up and headed back toward the stage. "Well, go home and get some rest, Pru. I'll want you fresh tonight, real fresh. You love to work? Well, so do I. So we'll work."

Laura got up, thinking she might as well get back to the hotel, too. "May I give you a lift, Miss Drake?"

The Amazon smiled. The smile was devoid of all animosity, and was actually quite warm and friendly. "That would be kind, Miss Staley. But please call me Pru. So you like my work, do you?"

"That bit, anyway."

"You must come watch us this evening, Miss Staley. I guarantee you'll see genius in action. Frank is a genius, you know. He made Julie Trotter the figure she is. And there are others I could name, big motion-picture stars now."

It excited Laura, and that excitement sparkled in her wide-spaced gray eyes. "Would you mind?"

"Why, I'd love it."

"Of course Ken Albright would be with me. We have a wonderful arrangement. Two or three evenings a week he has dinner with Dad and me, and then he has to reciprocate by taking me to dinner. I'm sure I get the better of the arrangement, but who am I to complain?"

"Oh, I don't object to having him watch me at rehearsal. He's a very nice boss. He doesn't expect genius for the salary he pays us. You're seeing a great deal of him, aren't you?"

Laura shrugged. One fellow was as good as another, and perhaps Ken Albright offered just a bit more. Certainly it was better than sitting home, night after night, just stewing and brooding like the Players' brooding Hamlet.

Very gently, Pru Drake said: "Of course I didn't mean to pry. Please forgive me, Miss Staley."

"Laura will do."

"It's a lovely name."

"Perhaps I do see more of him than I should. But perhaps it really doesn't matter."

Pru chuckled. "Everything matters, at least to an actress. Take that refugee part I play. I boned up on that. I think I've read every scrap printed about the atrocities committed by the Germans when they were less humble and 'democratic' than they are now. You read this, you do that, and bit by bit the small, the seemingly unimportant, becomes big. But you'll see tonight. Frank's so kind, isn't he?"

So, thought Laura, was lovely Pru Drake. How deftly and kindly she could change a subject!

She told Ken that while they were driving out to the barn that evening. "Really?" he asked.

"Really."

"But how did you know," he asked, "that she wasn't just playing a part?"

"She's not that good an actress."

"You don't think so?"

"I know so."

Yet that night, watching Pru up on the stage, she wondered if she knew anything at all about actresses. Frank, it seemed, had changed his mind about rehearsing the death scene. Now the Jewish refugee woman was living in one of the teeming slum streets of New York's lower East Side. She had just come in from the street, a potted geranium in her hands. The potted geranium, it developed, had been the gift of the Irish cop who patroled that street, and it was Pru's assignment to convey to the audience her delight with the gift and her amazement that a policeman could be so human, such a modest and humble democrat.

Again, Pru worked without benefit of costume or props. "Begin," Frank ordered, and Pru began cold. "Mrs. Green," she called, "such a wonderment. Look, Mrs. Green, will you look?"

And slowly, artfully, with no flaws that Laura could detect, she built up the scene into something so warm and human and realistic that Laura felt tears start to her eyes. Later, back in the car with Ken, she shook her head humbly. "I know nothing," she said. "I know nothing at all about actresses."

"Like her?"

"Didn't you?"

"She has talent. She'll be an apprentice for several years yet, however. Incidentally, Julie Trotter once played that role. Actually, she created it. And in that particular scene, Miss Laura Staley, everything was conveyed by Julie with her voice and her eyes."

"But people do run around like that when they're excited. And they do squeal and giggle and even cry. I liked it."

"Didn't you think it was somewhat hammy?"

"I did not!"

"Well, what was Mrs. Green doing all that time?"

"Why, she wasn't there!"

Ken laughed softly. "That, you see, is the point. A good actress, Laura, would have made you think Mrs. Green was there."

"But — but —"

"Oh, let's eat. Steamed clams again, over by the ocean?"

"Wonderful."

"By the way, since you are interested, why don't you attend all Pru's rehearsals? You'll discover something few people do — that acting isn't just taking bows."

"May I?"

He glanced down at her face in the moonlight. "You're a strange person, Laura. One moment you're a woman; the next moment you're a child."

Was that, she wondered, one of the reasons her romance had gone smash? Had she asked too much of Brad, as children did? Had she expected too much?

"Sure," he said easily. "Attend all the rehearsals you wish. And ask whatever questions you wish. There, does that make you happy?"

Oddly, it did. Laura didn't hesitate to tell him so, nor did she hesitate to attend the rehearsals, particularly those private and instructive rehearsals that involved Pru Drake. It was, she discovered, a grand way to fill in a few hours each day. It made a pleasant routine, indeed. Work at the hotel, dinner with her father and Ken, or just Ken alone, then off to the barn-theater for the show. Mrs. Bennett disapproved, of course. With the freedom of a woman who'd practically raised her from tadpole size, Mrs. Bennett said in the kitchen one evening: "You running from something, honey?"

"Running?"

"Since when did you become interested in the theater?"

"Since one was established in Saunder's Bluff."

"What about the Club work? What about the work right here? Anyway, you're not behaving like a Staley. You think different, ask anyone. Ask Mr. O'Neil."

"That old gossip?"

"Just the same —"

"And what am I supposed to do — sit here every night and brood?"

"So you are running away."

Laura flushed, perceiving the trap too late. "Anyway," she said stiffly, "I'm having fun."

"Well, I don't like it. All you and Brad Holbrook had was a spat. It should've been patched up by now. But here you are gallivanting with Ken Albright, and there Brad is gallivanting with that Helene Otis."

"He is?"

"Why look so surprised, so annoyed?"

Laura turned away, because Mrs. Bennett's sharp and knowing eyes were embarrassing. "Oh," she said crossly, "it doesn't matter."

"Isn't Mr. Albright engaged to that actress?"

"It was just a publicity stunt."

"Oh? My, but the younger generation works fast! He came here early in May. Just about two months later you and him are talking about engagements."

Laura swished out. She knew that if she hadn't she'd have said things she'd have regretted later on. She went angrily up to her bedroom, and stood brooding at her window until the first flames of anger had cooled.

CHAPTER 11

The big day of the theater opening came and Saunder's Bluff was ready for it. The streets were decorated with American flags and bunting. The Fire Department Band arrived early in the Common and enlivened the warm summer air with stirring marches. There was a parade along George Washington Avenue. There was a speech by Mayor Wolfe, who was in fine voice, and from three until six there was a great picnic to welcome the tourists to "the finest little town in all New England." For the merchants it was a gala day. The bells of their cash registers didn't play stirring marches, but they did play a tune that stirred the merchants. "The biggest thing ever!" Mr. O'Neil shouted to Laura above the hubbub resounding through the hotel lobby, and even Mr. Williston, the sulky deposed manager, unbent to the extent of saying to his successor: "I must say this is pretty fine." Laura, doing a tour of duty with him behind the desk, was inclined to agree. She could have sold twice the number of rooms the hotel boasted, and at twice the rental fees she was charging. And everyone else was making money, too. She wagged her head as Ken Albright came pushing through a crowd of well-wishers. "You should have demanded a free theater," she told him. "Why, if you were to ask for one now you'd get it Johnny-quick."

"Julie here?"

Laura gaped.

"She said she's coming. I ought to break her neck. She does a matinee and an evening show on Saturdays."

"I certainly haven't seen her."

"Well, if you do see her tell her I'm over at the theater. What time shall I pick you up?"

"I'm not going."

"What?"

Laura inhaled deeply and shouted over the bedlam: "I'm not going! I've given my ticket to Mrs. Bennett!"

Just then he was engulfed in still another tide of shouting and hearty well-wishers.

Tired of the noise, the commotion, Laura retreated to her office. Her face red and damp, her hair mussed, she shook her head ruefully at Mrs. Brigham. "If this is a sample of what will happen every weekend, we'll have to hire an extra pair of hands."

"Humph. A lot of that crowd isn't spending

money here. They're just hanging around to be in the middle of all the excitement."

"Is there excitement?"

"Very unfunny, Laura Staley. Very. And by the way, what do we do about the Players? They're all cooped up in their rooms upstairs. And Miss Ewing telephoned down to say that if they didn't eat pretty soon they'd all collapse from starvation."

"Send their food up. Mr. Albright's determined to keep them out of sight until curtain-time."

"Send up what, and with whom? Oh, and that reminds me. Our chef threatens to quit if she isn't given more help."

"Glory!"

Laura hustled through the crowded lobby and through the crowded, old-fashioned dining-room to the kitchen. She was wearing one of her better faille dresses, but she rolled up her sleeves anyway and grinned encouragingly at the very flustered Mrs. Monihan. "Me darlin'," she crooned, " 'tis that proud of yez that I am now. 'Tis indade a miracle yez have been standin' up under the burden."

"No soft soap!"

" 'Tis only me foine Mrs. Monihan as could've done it."

"Whist, I'm deef."

"An' never a complaint, an' that hard she's workin', too."

"Complaint! If it wasn't as there isn't so many they confuse me, I'd be talkin' meself black an' blue."

"Could I be helpin' yez, now?"

"With me wages."

"Ha-ha, will yez be listenin' t' the poor lady rant? But I know better, that I do."

"Girl, it's too old I am. An' now all them stage people is after me for their dinners."

Laura shrugged. "Ah, let's feed them. I'll do theirs, and you sit down and rest your bones. We'll broil some steaks, we'll give them French fried potatoes and a nice salad. That'll do."

"For the blessed income of twenty-two dollars a week, now, an' with rooms thrown in at that?"

"Mrs. Monihan, we're sold out! And we'll be sold out Thursdays, Fridays, Saturdays and Sundays throughout the summer. Why, we're making so much money I've decided to raise your salary twenty per cent."

"Well, now!"

"Just for the season, of course."

"Such a foine, foine girl as it is. Me darlin', will yez please sit yourself down an' watch me workin' in me gratitude?"

Laura did the steaks, however, while Mrs.

Monihan did the salads. She then commandeered the services of several of the waitresses in the dining-room and took the dinner trays upstairs. And there she found such peace, such quiet she was startled. A couple of card games were in progress in the small third-floor sitting-room. In several of the bedrooms the girls were washing their clothes or writing a few postcards, and there were two who were actually sleeping.

Her surprise must have shown, because in his room John Grover, the brooding Hamlet, the male lead of the first play, laughed. "Stage fright, Miss Staley?"

"Well, haven't you?"

He gestured casually. "It's a profession, just like any profession. Oh, I suppose I'm a bit on edge. But if you know your job, why be nervous?"

With Pru, she discovered, it was quite different. The Amazon was stretched out on her bed, attractive as always in the eternal shorts and T-shirt, but so tense and nervous she was trembling. "Will you get that tray out of here?" she snapped. "And you get out, too! Always around! Always spying! Why don't you mind your own business?"

Laura gestured, and the shocked waitress did leave with the offending tray of food. But understanding Pru, Laura just closed the door and went over to the opened window. From that coign of vantage she had a good view of the crowds of tourists exploring that section of Saunder's Bluff. She also had a good view of the distant mountains and farmland.

"What do you see?" Pru Drake asked. "Good heavens, what's there in this pumpkin center to see?"

"People and scenery. Miss Trotter's coming, Pru."

"She's a ham. She is so!"

Laura turned and smiled at the poor flushed, tense face. "I know. Did you know that Frank Jones said just the other day that in another two years you'll make people forget Julie Trotter?"

"He did?"

"Mr. Albright didn't agree, but —"

"What does he know? He's just a fellow who inherited a lot of money. So he's a producer, but what does he know about acting? Anyway, he's so in love with Julie Trotter it's pathetic."

Laura started.

Pru laughed, and the sounds of her laughter were oddly like the sounds of breaking glass. "No, he didn't tell you that, did he? Look, you're a good kid. I didn't think so, but I've changed my mind. And you're trying to help me now, and I appreciate it, so I'll return the favor. You're just another country girl to Ken Albright. But when we go back to New York he'll go back, too, and it'll be to that ham actress."

"Easy does it, Pru."

"I hate her! What's she coming here for, to criticize my performance?"

"Perhaps to learn, Pru."

The blonde gasped. She stood up, almost a foot taller than Laura, but so beautifully proportioned she didn't seem so tall, so big. "To learn? From me?"

Laura gave her bare arm a little pat. "You once told me at rehearsal that a person can learn from anyone. Well, if you can learn by studying people, why can't she learn by studying you?"

The blonde nodded. The logic of that seemed to have cut through the fog of nervousness and fear, to have reached the core of her brain. "Dear," she cooed, and she was more like herself, "how sweet you can be!"

And that, Laura thought, was all she or anyone else could do for the young actress. She gave the girl's arm another pat and went back to the third-floor sitting-room. Everyone was in there except Pru and the sleepers, each chomping away happily. The sassy redhead gave her a beaming glance. "Miss Staley," she said, "any time you want Helene Otis poisoned, you come to me."

Helene was indignant. "That's mean. Miss Staley, I assure you my interest in your Brad Holbrook was purely business. Why, the idea!"

They were kids, Laura decided. Their talent made them special, but they were kids for all that. She thought it was amazing that Frank Jones could keep them under control, and that Ken Albright could actually build a going concern around them.

"Quite all right," she assured Helene. "I'll have coffee sent up in a little bit. But no dessert. Mr. Albright said he didn't want any of you filling up on anything sweet. I wonder why."

No one answered, because that was when Pru came out.

The reactions were several, and interesting. Sally Ewing bustled about like a mother hen, getting Pru comfortably seated. John Grover found the tray Pru had refused. Ronnie Case, seeming to forget his grudge against Pru, promptly assured her that she'd never been lovelier. Only Helene Otis retained her coolness toward Pru and her air of wishing that Pru worked somewhere else. For better or worse, the general attitude seemed to be, Pru was one of them and was entitled to their active and moral support.

Nice kids, Laura thought, going back downstairs to the excitement and bedlam. Wonderful kids! If they weren't a smash hit it would be a shame, because they certainly deserved to be, all of them, and Frank and Ken deserved it, too!

She found a gangling fellow waiting in her office, a fellow with a totally bald head, a fellow wearing tortoise-shell, thick-lensed glasses. He got up, made a perfunctory bow. "I'm Manny Cohen, Miss Staley. Albright's business manager."

"How nice to meet you, Mr. Cohen. Ken's told me a great deal about you."

"He kept it polite, I trust?"

"Very polite and very warm, Mr. Cohen."

"Well, I love him, too. He's a screwball, I won't deny that. Still, he's fine. Where's Julie?"

"I wouldn't know. Has she come?"

Manny Cohen spoke wearily because he was weary. He was weary of temperamental stars. He was weary of women who asked silly questions. He was also weary of standing — and sat down. "When you see me," he stated, "you should see Julie Trotter, too. This is not levity. This woman called Julie Trotter, in civilized circles, that is, happens to be better than an investment in any company you can name. And a business manager is always around the big investment. Only she gave me the slip, mentioning a cottage small by some bucolic waterfall."

Laura laughed softly, happily, beginning to feel excited. "Well, I know where she is then, Mr. Cohen. I'll send her to you."

"You're a pretty kid."

"All of me thanks you, Mr. Cohen."

He grinned. "Snappy tongue, too. I hear tell you've been seen here and there with the boss."

"Would you rather have Miss Trotter, or a date by date description of my scandalous affair with Mr. Albright?"

"Real sense of humor. Love it. Would love Julie more. I'll be in the restaurant for the next hour or so. All right?"

Laura said it was all right, and drove home, inching her way through the traffic, so excited now she was beginning to tremble. At home she changed into slacks and a blouse and bummed a picnic hamper of food from Mrs. Bennett in the kitchen. Then she got back into her car and drove south toward the outskirts of Saunder's Bluff. She halted her car at the end of the paved road and got out and methodically tested the dirt road that ran farther on through the small clump of woods toward Corkscrew Creek. Having found it firm, she got back into her car and drove on, admiring the birches and beeches and willows, admiring the bird calls flashing through the afternoon air, admiring the peace and quiet of the setting. She gave a warning beep as she rounded the turn, and then when she'd parked her car near the split-rail fence that surrounded the cottage yard, she just leaned out the window and hailed.

Softly melodious laughter sounded on her left. There was a moment of silence, and then Julie Trotter came around a clump of bushes, her black eyes lovely and alert. She smiled beautifully, but with an odd shyness that went straight to Laura's heart. "You're Laura, of course," she said. "How nice. And what a lovely place this is. I told your father I couldn't quite believe my good fortune."

"Hungry, Miss Trotter? I've brought all sorts of things for you to eat. Oh, and Mr. Cohen is very anxious to find you."

Julie Trotter wrinkled her nose. "Pfui on Manny. I don't intend to stir an inch from this delightful, sequestered place until curtain time. My, how lovely you are, Miss Laura Staley."

"You're very kind, Miss Trotter."

"Nonsense. Now, then, shall we have ourselves a nice picnic? Oh, do stop blushing and staring, dear; I'm quite real and quite human."

Laura swallowed. So this, she thought, was

what a star was in the flesh. And this was what Pru Drake would become, a creature to hold the eye, with a personality so strong it caught and held your attention like a magnet.

Julie Trotter took the picnic hamper from her hand. She turned and gracefully strolled back the way she had come, and Laura followed. She found that Julie had laid one of their better blankets on the ground near the creek. It troubled her somewhat, and the great actress seemed to sense that.

"You don't mind, do you, that I've been using one of your old blankets for a groundcover? All my life I've been frightened of bugs. I hate them so, don't you?"

"Oh, that's all right. Here, why don't you let me sit you down and do the serving? It's fine having you here, Miss Trotter."

Was she wrong, or did those beautiful, jet black eyes narrow ever so faintly?

"I wish I could have seen you in that play they're doing tonight, Miss Trotter," she tried again. "Mr. Albright tells me you were superb in it."

"I'm always superb. It's my business to be. Now, then, with the formalities out of the way, shall we be ourselves?"

Laura stared. "But aren't we?"

"I wonder. However, I shall give you the benefit of the doubt. But after I say, Laura, that Ken Albright is in love with me and engaged to me, what do you say, eh?"

Laura studied the babbling, sparkling, swirling creek. "I'd say that was your business, I believe. And I still say it's wonderful to have you here. Golly, we'll call this Julie Trotter Cottage."

Julie Trotter nodded. "I do hope I haven't been mistaken in my judgment of your sweet character, Laura. Well, we shall see. In the meantime, shall we get acquainted?"

Laura felt uneasy. She didn't like that glitter deep in Julie Trotter's black eyes.

She heard herself saying something she'd never expected to say. She heard herself saying lamely: "Well, I'd better get back to town."

She heard something more as she rushed back to her car. She heard Julie Trotter laughing. Or was she wrong? Was it just the tinkling sound of the creek flowing on in its ancient way under the ancient sun?

CHAPTER 12

The next two weeks were among the most confusing weeks Laura had ever spent in her life. She never had a second chat with Julie Trotter at the cottage. The star remained only to attend the grand opening of the Albright Country Theater. When Laura went to the cottage the next morning to invite Julie Trotter to the house for breakfast, she found Frank sitting alone on the little porch, smoking a fat cigar. He smiled in his amiable way, and half-rose, but sat right down again. "Julie is like the night," he stated. "Julie comes and goes, comes and goes. Did you think Pru did a good job?"

"I wasn't there."

"Smart girl. People who attend opening nights never do get the chance to bother with a mere play. Well, for the record, Pru did a darned good job."

"How wonderful."

"I accept your hearty congratulations."

Laura laughed. She liked Frank Jones. The

more she saw of him the better she liked him, perhaps because he was so human. "Well," she joshed, "you were pretty good, too."

"But let's face it," Frank Jones said. "That blonde has all the instincts of a hungry tigress. She can't help clawing because it's her nature to claw."

"Does it matter what she is? You forget all that, it seems to me, when she's on stage."

"I find it difficult to work with a tigress."

"But she's so convinced you're a genius, Frank, that I think she'd speak her lines standing on her head if you were to suggest it."

The wrinkled, middle-aged face became an enormous scowl. "Yes, I guess she would, at that. Did you know the boss has went?"

Laura was surprised. No, she hadn't known. It had been her intention to invite Ken to the house for breakfast, too. She gazed around at the small fenced yard. She noticed that the grass needed cutting, that the flower-beds needed weeding. She must send their gardener over, she thought.

"Big row," Frank explained. "It began backstage during intermission. Julie decided at the last minute that she wanted to do the third act. Big gesture. Once a ham always a ham. But Pru wouldn't budge. Real thrill."

Laura guessed the rest, or thought she had. "So there was a bigger row, and Pru's no longer connected with the troupe?"

"Well, so far she's a member of the troupe, but in very, very bad standing. You might say that she won't be given another lead for weeks, if ever."

Now Laura understood why he was sitting there all alone, with sadness deep in his eyes. A sentimental man, this stocky, fatherly director. He loved the world and he loved the world's people. He wanted everyone to be happy, and he was unhappy when everyone wasn't. And Pru had been his project. He'd worked darned hard with Pru because he'd admired the girl's determination to succeed and he'd respected her willingness to work, to seek improvement.

"Big row," Frank Jones continued. "You might say that I talked too much. I do that. Like sitting here right this minute and telling you that when the summer's over Ken will go back to New York."

Laura reached down and picked up a twig and traced a picture in the dirt. "Am I in love with him, Frank?"

"Not definitely, to answer precisely. I think you were hurt by Holbrook, and Ken was around, very sympathetic, and his sympathy pleased you. I think you could be, though. I like you, apple-seed. You like the theater, so I like you. Yes, and I guess I like you for the way you treat your employees at the hotel. I see things. Real eyes."

"I think you're mistaken, Frank."

"Apple-seed?"

"Don't call me that, please. Frank, do you know anything about me? I've been properly educated. To a man like my father, travel is an integral part of anyone's education. Frank, I've seen many of the countries abroad. I've seen much of this country. If I prefer to live in Saunder's Bluff it's because I love Saunder's Bluff, not because I'm limited in my knowledge of the world, or in my outlook."

"Hey, are you rich?"

Laura smiled sunnily. "Very rich. But we don't attach much importance to wealth here, Frank. Why should we why should anyone?"

"When you say rich, do you mean ten bucks above your debts, or what?"

"When I say rich I mean I'm rich in friends, I hope, and in respect and even in love. Dad has more than a million, I think, if you're referring to money."

He let his breath out with a swoosh. "Even when you say it fast it's more than I have. Funny thing about me. I make good money. It goes, though, I don't know why. Anyway, it figures, then. I just thought Julie was making a big fuss."

"Oh?"

"Accusation: Just because Laura Staley has position and money you're making a fool of yourself. Accusation: Just because you've grown foolish on the subject of New England you're ready to forget New York and all of us in it. Accusation: You've become as stupid, as downright stupid, as these hicks. Yup, I thought it was just big talk."

Laura drew her brows together over her short, lovely nose. "But what did all that have to do with Pru Drake?"

"Helene Otis has been writing letters to Julie. A little arrangement they made. And Helene Otis wanted the part Pru played, and so it got to Julie that Pru was given the part because you liked Pru and Ken was playing up to you. Amusing?"

Laura wanted to go to the hotel and slap Helene Otis on the face!

"You get the point?" Frank Jones asked.

"I think so. The purpose of all this was to make me feel somewhat guilty. I am now to try to help Pru. Which I'll do, of course. And I'm supposed to come of age, to realize Ken Albright is just playing, and kiss and make up with Brad?"

He leaned forward and gave her shoulder a little pat. "Believe me, youngster, you'll be happier if you do."

Disturbed, Laura went back to the house.

She pained her father by announcing Julie Trotter had left, and she further pained him by announcing Ken Albright had left with her. "Hang it," her father growled, "I was looking forward to entertaining Miss Trotter."

"She makes me sick!"

Mr. Staley threw back his semi-bald head. "What's that?"

Laura didn't elaborate; there was too little time. The bell rang, and the caller was the brooding Hamlet, John Grover. Having won seven curtain calls the night before, John Grover was now a smiling, handsome young man. "Nice to see you, John. You look very well rested for a fellow who probably didn't get to bed until early this morning."

"Grand, just grand. Say, how about going for a ride with me in the jalopy? You may as well know, Laura, that you'll have to say yes. All the other town girls have been warned about actors, it seems."

"Well, why not?"

"This from you?"

"I meant, why wouldn't I go? It'd be fun."

It was, too. He did talk a great deal about himself, and he did talk a great deal about his undeniably great ability, and he did suggest she was fortunate to be in his company, but aside from little things like that he was great fun. They went all the way to the seacoast and went swimming. They had a wonderful lunch right out on the beach, and then he located a miniature golf course and proceeded to demonstrate that at least some of his time had been spent mastering something other than his art. They returned to Saunder's Bluff barely in time for him to get made up for his part. "Fine fun," he yelled, dashing for the stage door, "really fine fun!"

The next afternoon it was Ronnie Case who came calling. The little fellow, quick and bright and sassy as any bird, declared he was pained. "Miss Staley," he said, "I ask you: Why should John have all the dates? True, he's handsome. True, he has talent. Still, am I less human than he is?"

And so she went out with Mr. Ronnie Case. Mr. Ronnie Case was the male comedian and he took his reputation for being a good one very, very seriously. He had a great fund of jokes, which he tapped. He had a keen eye for the whimsical, which he proved. But like Johnny Grover before him, Mr. Ronnie Case also liked Mr. Ronnie Case. But Laura forgave him when she discovered that his idea of fun was a horseback ride through the hills. The instant she was in the saddle she felt better. Brad ceased to matter, as did Julie Trotter and all her other problems. She gazed back over her shoulder and whooped: "I'll race you to the top of that hill."

Ronnie gave a yip of encouragement to his horse, and the race was on.

Ronnie won the race very easily.

"You bounce too much," he said. "That wears your horse out. Did I neglect to tell you I almost became a jockey?"

"Really, Ronnie?"

"Here, let me teach you to ride, Miss Staley."

She was bone-weary when he finally decided he'd kept her practicing long enough. That night she went to bed early, with Mrs. Bennett there to give her a massaging and a scolding.

"Honey," Mrs. Bennett said, "I don't understand you."

"I don't either. Ouch, I've broken a bone!"

"Actors and producers and actors. And all the time Brad acting foolish, too. Now he's going around with that blonde."

"I really don't care, Mrs. Bennett."

"All he's trying to do is earn money."

"Lordy, will you forget all that?"

"You sure aren't a Staley or a Saunder. You forget pretty quick."

Did it matter? Laura wondered.

She fell asleep early, but that was the only night during the rest of July that she did. It seemed as if all the male members of the Albright Players had decided to give her a rush.

One by one they came, and when they didn't either Sally Ewing or Helene Otis did.

"What we're all trying to do," Sally explained, "is show our appreciation for all the kind things you do for us."

Helene Otis put it differently. "You know, Miss Staley, you're sweet. And we thought if there's anything we could do to give you some fun we'd like to do it."

Such as writing tattletale letters to Julie Trotter? Laura wondered.

"And anyway," Sally said another time, "we think that if anyone can help Pru get out of the doghouse you can. Sure, she was out of line. I mean, in this business you can think a big star is a ham, but you haven't the right to call her one."

"Pru *did?*"

"Sure she did."

"Well, what do you know?"

Sally answered literally, her dark green eyes flashing. "I know Pru was right. But in this business being right doesn't count."

CHAPTER 13

In New York, in West Eleventh Street, in the spacious, air-conditioned living-room of Julie Trotter's house, Ken Albright sat sitting before the candy-stone fireplace, waiting for Julie to come downstairs. She was, he was thinking, the silliest woman he had ever starred in a play. She was on top. Frank had taught her well and she'd learned her lessons well, and she was a glorious star with a glorious career ahead of her. Yet for an illusion of love she was quite prepared to toss the career aside, as if her career didn't matter a jot. Yet into that career she had put her all. Yet for that career she'd worked and schemed, even as Prudence Drake up in Saunder's Bluff was doing now. Silly? No, Ken thought, it was worse than plain silliness. He'd used a weak word. The word he should have used was —

He turned, rose. He put on a charming smile and went across the room to bow over Julie's hand. "Delightful," he murmured. "Julie, you're so lovely you could just stand there on the stage without speaking a word — and win encores."

"Very glib. I'm cross with you. Do you know how cross with you I am?"

"Surely you don't mean that, Julie."

"Ken, I tell you this frankly: if I weren't in love with you I'd never forgive you. That poor child. Why, she positively trembled with awe when she saw me. No, she can't be blamed. She's to be pitied, the poor child. But you?"

"Julie, you mustn't become overwrought. You know you do your best work when you —"

"Have you fired that impertinent apprentice?"

"No, Julie, I haven't."

"Ken, I warn you. There are limits. Please don't drive me into a nervous breakdown."

"To punish her for her impertinence, however, I have demoted her, and I have instructed Frank to keep her inactive for a time."

The black eyes blazed. "I demand that she be fired!"

"Julie, compose yourself."

Julie Trotter whirled. She darted to the telephone on the handsome cherry table. She pointed a quivering forefinger at it melodramatically. "Use it," she ordered. "Telephone

Frank in that tank town at once. Tell him to fire her."

The difficulty, Ken thought, was that the well-being of so many in the Broadway play was dependent upon this silly woman before him. She was box-office. To the public she was all winsome charm and beauty. The play would stagger along without her name to pull the customers in, but the take would be small, so small that sooner or later the owner of the theater would regretfully announce he'd have to book it to another company. Yes, there was the rub. If it weren't for the others in the play, Ken thought, he'd battle it out with Julie now.

"Let's do it this way," he said. "Sleep on it for a week. If at the end of that time you still want her discharged, just tell me so and it will be done."

She knew her strength. "Now."

Did it matter? Ken asked himself. Who was Prudence Drake? Why should he be so concerned about her? Yes, she had talent. She could be a star one day if she continued to work hard, to develop, and if she had luck. But couldn't that be said of many in the company up there? John Grover was an up-and-coming star. Sally Ewing. Helene Otis. Given time, training, opportunity — what difference would it make, actually, if just one among them was shouldered out into the wings? He owed Pru nothing. But he did owe his company here on Broadway a great deal. They had worked hard to perfect their skills, and because of that he had a smash hit on his hands that would be good for another year where it was and for several years out on the road. So why worry about Pru Drake? The girl had asked for it, hadn't she?

"Well, Ken, will you or won't you make that call?"

But on the other hand, Ken thought, Pru was a human being, for all her foibles, her frailties. She had worked hard, and was entitled to her chance. She had been baited and badgered by Julie, and had been entitled to hit back. And what about that good old American principle of fair play?

"Ken, will you stop standing there daydreaming?"

Ken nodded. For better or worse, he had made up his mind. He went to the cherry table and reached for the telephone. "Very well," he said cheerfully, "I'll break her heart."

"The snip."

"And I'll never see you again, Julie. That, too, is a promise.

"Ken!"

He got the long-distance operator and carefully gave her the number of the Staley Hotel in Saunder's Bluff, Vermont. Julie nodded, and stepped back from the table.

"That's better, Ken. Now after you've dealt with her I want to discuss the play I'll do for you up there."

His handsome face remained grim, almost stony.

"Ken, didn't you hear me?"

"I heard you."

"Well, give a smile; say something."

"You won't ever play for me again, Julie."

"Ken!"

Into the telephone he said: "Frank Jones, please. This is Kenneth Albright calling."

"Ken, does she mean something to you, too? How many girls have you been flirting with up there while I've been working so hard in this stinking, humid city?"

"That you, Frank? Sure, I love you, too. Frank, be a pal, will you, and cut Pru Drake's throat? No. Please don't protest, Frank. I have no choice. Julie wants her pound of flesh, and I'm giving it to her."

"Don't you dare blame me, Ken Albright! It's her own fault! The effrontery of that apprentice, calling me a ham!"

Ken hung up. His face was grayish, his blue eyes dull. His expression and color frightened Julie and she cried out, but Ken just turned and kept walking. He closed the street door so quietly behind him Julie barely heard it. And then Julie Trotter was really frightened. Had he meant it when he'd said he'd never see her again?

Good heavens!

Julie rushed out to the heat and humidity of West Eleventh Street. But by then, of course, Ken had gotten into his Cadillac roadster and had driven away. . . .

The sentimental man played with the notion of quitting. The rich girl liked him, he figured, so if it came to a question of eating money she'd find him a job doing something that would get him the money he needed. He'd been in the theater too long. It wasn't fun any more. You made a star and the star turned into green cheese. You found good material from which to fashion another star, and an otherwise nice guy told you to take a knife and cut that material's throat. Maybe he should've quit last year, while he'd still had a dime in the bank.

"Boo!"

The sentimental man grimaced. "Sally," he said, "kid stuff is for kids. A good comedian's an adult who thinks like an adult and who's very funny and paid big dough because his jokes and antics are adult. Yoo, hoo, come out, come out, wherever you are."

Sally joined the sentimental man on the bench before the red-boarded, white-battened barn-theater. "You sound bitter, Pops."

"Is that a gopher, that cute fellow with his head sticking up from the ground?"

"It's a field mouse. How beautiful the country is. See the mountains or hills or whatever they call them. Have you noticed that Johnny Appleseed is building up a goodly crop of something or other for a goodly harvest?"

"Vegetables," Frank Jones said disgustedly. "Me, I'm a meat man, myself."

"Who's running that tractor? Ha, ha, I thought for a moment it was the Viking marooned in New England."

"She's pretty, that kid, you know?"

"Unfortunately, I do know. I don't understand her, Frank. She makes with the cutlass for John and I hate her. She makes with the dagger for the star, and I love her. Now there she's going pumpkins and beans for the dobbin, and I have no views to speak of. May I tell you my views?"

"What are they, Sally — seriously?"

"Well, the way I've figured it out, speaking seriously, is that the Amazon works hard at whatever she does. She works hard to be an actress. She works hard to be the dear thing no rich guy can do without. She isn't one or the other yet, but she's in there developing all her talents, and you can't be really angry with her because only very humble people study as hard as she does."

"The dobbin likes her. She brings out the carrots in the dobbin."

"Honestly?"

"And that's unfortunate. It works this way. For my cash Miss Laura Staley loves the dobbin. And I was counting on Miss Laura Staley to save Pru Drake's future in the theater. But whoa! The dobbin fancies he's found his one and only, and where do we go from here?"

Sally blinked. "Well, where?"

"I have a job for you, Sally."

The pert redhead's body twitched. She stood up and thrust her hands into the slash pockets of her slacks. "I won't like this," she said, intuitively sad. "I won't like this a bit."

"Just go out to yonder Amazon, Sally, and tell her she's fired."

"It's unfair! I don't love the Amazon. But she works. And she never consciously steals scenes, either — not often, at any rate. She deserves better!"

"Just the same —"

"That Laura Staley! She promised to help Pru. I thought she was one of those honest reliable New Englanders."

"Just the same —"

"No."

"Thank you, Sally."

"Not until after I've talked with the others. If they say okay, then it's okay, I'll do it. If not, I won't."

When she'd gone back into the barn-theater, the sentimental man frowned. Well, he'd been given his orders. As long as he was accepting pay from Ken Albright it was his duty to obey all orders promptly and unquestioningly. So he should either do his duty, or quit. Yup, there it was, right on the line.

But it was hot out there where all those vegetables grew. A fellow could probably be knocked dead by sunstroke if he walked all the way across that field. A fellow had a duty to himself, too, didn't he?

"Dear boss," Frank croaked, miserable and sad, "I love you, too, but my mother never brought me up to be a louse."

When he got back to the hotel, he decided, he'd write a letter of resignation and send it to Manny in New York. . . .

Johnny Grover suggested that the Albright Players should use their God-given intelligence for a change. After all the talk, after all the arguments, after all the speeches, he said, no one was mentally fit enough to make an intelligent decision. "So let's be smart," he concluded, "and sleep on it the rest of the week. Hey, we have a play to put on, remember?"

Sally hotly countered: "The time to act is now!"

She was voted down, however, by a vote of ten to five, and no formal plans for action were drawn up until after they had put on their fourth play of the season. And that, it developed, was fortunate for Pru Drake. For the undeniable fact was that Helene Otis, switched to the lead role, lacked the ability of Pru and failed to please the audience. The play drew capacity crowds Thursday and Friday, since those were the nights when the season tickets were honored. But there was a sharp drop in attendance on Saturday, and the barn was three quarters empty on Sunday. Thus it was brought home to everyone that he had a personal interest in helping Pru, as well as a duty to fair play to do all he could do to bring Pru back into the fold.

Monday morning there was another meeting of the Albright Players, this time in the sitting-room of the third floor of the Staley Hotel. And now there were no arguments about what they would do. Now the only arguments involved method. It was Sally's belief, ringingly expressed, that a letter of protest be written at once and despatched to Ken Albright in New York. It was also Sally's belief, ringingly expressed, that Julie Trotter should be made aware of their determination to send the whole story to the New York City newspapers, if necessary. These suggestions were submitted to a vote and were carried unanimously.

The redhead's green eyes flashed gloriously. "And if that doesn't get action," she whooped, "darned if we don't go on strike!"

While she was typing the letters in her room, no less a personage than the Amazon came in to collect her belongings. Pru smiled sweetly, the only person who seemed to be unconcerned about the fact she'd been fired. "Dear Sally," she said, "you mustn't scowl so. Wrinkles appear, beauty fades, then a woman must go it on talent alone."

"You're looking well, Amazon."

"The country life is good for one. One drinks milk, eats fresh eggs, garden-fresh vegetables. One exercises, one sleeps soundly, one lives."

"Did you see the play?"

"I saw the play."

"A real dog, wasn't it?"

"To put it kindly, Helene Otis is about five years away from competency. She's good in musicals, I'll concede that. But the play wasn't a musical, was it?"

"Sit down, Amazon. I have news. None of

us loves you, as I'm sure you know, but we do respect your work and we do think it's a shame that you were fired. So we're sending a protest to the boss and we're threatening Julie Trotter with all kinds of very nasty publicity. We think we'll win, too."

"I see."

Pru Drake sat down. It was an almost liquid flow of her person to the chair, with none of the usual jerks, without noticeable effort. Sally was enchanted. "How can a big lug like you be so graceful?"

"Practice. Sally, did you know that I was born on a farm in Minnesota?"

"Amazon!"

"I did all types of farm work, Sally. I was very clumsy. And it didn't help that I was always reading plays, memorizing lines, practicing acting whenever I could. My father was the old-fashioned sort who seemed to think a good sound licking every two days would cure me. So I ran away. I worked as a waitress in Chicago. I went to acting school. After school I'd go home to my furnished room and I'd stand before the full-length mirror I'd bought and I'd practice until I was groggy. That's the only way, Sally. You must practice, practice, practice until all you do is done gracefully, until every gesture, every bit of timing is natural to you, a part of you."

"You've learned a lot, Amazon. You have twice the ability I have."

"But what good is it, Sally, if just one human being can come along and smash it all, just like that? It's no good at all, you see. Anything's better, even marriage to a farmer."

"Pru, stop talking like that."

Pru did. And she did something Sally had never thought she'd ever see the Amazon do. She suddenly burst into a hoarse sob. And the tears streaming from her eyes were genuine, too. . . .

CHAPTER 14

Laura, meanwhile, was enjoying that peace and quiet she had told John Grover she wanted. She formed the habit of spending just her mornings at the hotel, a practice that pleased the deposed manager Mr. Williston because it gave him the opportunity to exercise his authority as assistant manager, something he seemed to enjoy doing. Her afternoons were devoted to house affairs and to village affairs. Her evenings were spent with her father, or with Hazel, or with several other friends in that segment of the town. She tried to get to bed at ten o'clock at the latest. It was idiotic to stay up until all hours of the night, she told Hazel once, because you were so sleepy the next day you couldn't possibly enjoy yourself or your life. But the trouble was that while she did get into bed by ten more often than not, she had difficulty falling asleep. There were too many memories — memories of Brad and the good times she'd had with him, memories of Ken and his kindness and his understanding and the good times she'd had with him, too. Sometimes, alone there in the warm dark, she wondered if she shouldn't make one final effort with Brad, and on occasion the mere thought of doing so sent tingles down to her toes. Other times she wished fretfully that Ken Albright would return to Saunder's Bluff. Why was he staying in New York? Was he seeing the actress; was he as much in love with Julie as Julie seemed to think? And sleep, when it doddered along at last, offered little escape from these thoughts, because then her subconscious took over and spun dream after dream that involved one man or the other, and sometimes both.

This told.

It left her gray eyes somewhat dull, and it sometimes left puffy blue semicircles high up on either side of her short, lovely nose. One day Mrs. Bennett asked: "You off your feed, honey?" Another day her father asked: "Anything you want to talk over with me?" She was able to fend them off, but her friend, Hazel, who was Belle Adrian's daughter, and Mrs. Wolfe weren't quite as easy to handle. After lunch one afternoon Hazel said the dishes could wait and led Laura back into her small but very attractively furnished livingroom. "Sit down," Hazel ordered. "I'd like to talk to you. You'll find that green leather armchair comfortable, I'm sure."

Laura sat down listlessly.

Hazel sat down, a grinning, happy figure in a pink blouse and red play-shorts. She'd put on weight since her recent marriage, and her eyes seemed darker and greener than ever. Also, she'd changed the arrangement of her hair. Now it was cropped short in a poodle-dog fashion that left Hazel looking almost as pert and sassy as another redhead Laura knew.

"Stewing," Hazel announced, "never helps. And you've been stewing, Laura, haven't you?"

"Not really. I mean, I have no regrets. Oh, I sometimes think back to spring, to how happy I was, to how sure I was that all my golden dreams would come true. And that leaves me somewhat depressed. But I don't regret having ended my engagement, if that's what you mean. Brad didn't want marriage as such. It was silly to go on as I was going."

"I was talking," Hazel explained gently, "about Ken Albright. Did you know that one fine evening I had Ken here for dinner, and that we spent most of the evening discussing your many attractions?"

Laura started. A hungry expression came into her eyes.

"He's a very nice boy," Hazel said with satisfaction. "Joe liked him, too. He's very human, Ken Albright is. Here's what I mean. My husband's just a factory worker. That's nothing to be ashamed of, because it's honest work and Joe's a good worker. But a lot of people in Ken Albright's position would have the idea they're better than Joe. Ken didn't. They sat there talking as equals, and it wasn't being put on by Ken; you can tell about such things. Yes, it was a fine evening."

"He's a fine man."

"What did he say about you? Oh, a lot of things. He said it made him comfortable to be near you. He said one of the nicest things about you was that you could take a licking like a real lady. He said that Brad Holbrook had been very foolish, because the fellow who married you would be marrying a very fine person. He had a lot of nice things like that to say about you."

It came tearing from Laura's lips; she couldn't help it. "And he went back to New York, to stay!"

Hazel nodded wisely. "You've been stewing about that, haven't you?"

"And this terrible thing he's done to Pru Drake. The theater was everything to Pru Drake. And just like that, for no reason to speak of, he ordered her to be fired."

"Don't you think he's a fair and decent guy?"

If she weren't positive of that, Laura thought, she'd not be "stewing!" "Oh, of course he is. But this Julie Trotter seems to have him under her control. She seems able to force him to do whatever she wants him to do."

"Anyway, Laura, why stew? If he's at all important to you, you should be feeling glad. If he isn't, you shouldn't be thinking about him at all."

It was at that point that Mayor Wolfe rang in her unofficial capacity as Hazel's friend. "I demand entrance," she called, "lest I perspire down into globs."

Hazel's lovely legs flashed into action, and presently Mayor Wolfe was established in the green leather armchair. Because the chair was so comfortable Mayor Wolfe glanced benignly at Laura. "It was very nice of you," she said, "to give Hazel and Joe such a fine present."

Laura grinned faintly. "When you marry Mr. King, Mrs. Wolfe, I'll buy you one, too."

"Hazel, did you hear? You're my witness!"

Laughing gaily, Hazel went out to the kitchen to make some iced tea. While she was gone Mayor Wolfe took advantage of this golden opportunity she had to snoop. "Something wrong, Laura?"

"Oh, it's just this weather. I'm a frost-on-the-punkin girl, myself."

"I'm very glad, Laura, that that pressure we once discussed hasn't backfired."

How long ago it was, thought Laura. Measured the conventional way, of course, it wasn't long ago at all. But measured in terms of events, in things felt, in thoughts hatched, it seemed years and years ago.

"Speaking of pressure," Mayor Wolfe said, "did you know the Albright Players intend to apply pressure to Mr. Albright? I was approached by that cute comedian, Sally Ewing. She wanted me to help. I don't know if I should have felt as flattered as I did. We politicians like you voters to believe we don't even know the meaning of the word pressure. A good politician conceals the fact that he does. Anyway —"

"Have you seen their last two plays?"

"I concede that Pru Drake was the glue that held everything together. You know, that astonishes me. I see her parading her lovely legs up and down our streets, I contemplate the size of her, the ferocity of her, and I'm amazed to think she's an actress. And when I recall how beautifully she played the role of that Jewish refugee — well!"

"I don't blame them," Laura said. "It just isn't fair."

Mayor Wolfe shrugged. Hazel came in with three glasses of iced tea tinkling on the sterling-silver tray the Mayor had given her for a wedding gift. Hazel had poured the tea into very gay tumblers, and Hazel served a gay napkin as she served the tea. She seemed to take great pride in doing things properly, carefully; and studying her as she sat down, Laura decided that Hazel was the happiest of them all because Hazel had the important things — and knew it. She held her glass high. "To the lovely housewife in her lovely home," she toasted. She raised the glass to her lips — and that was when the idea came bursting into her mind.

She was so startled she cried out.

The women stared.

Her eyes big and round, Laura stared back. "Of course," she muttered, "of course."

Mayor Wolfe said caustically, "Oh, have you finally gotten my point?"

Greatly excited, coming alive, fully alive, suddenly, Laura returned her glass to the silver tray. She turned and went briskly toward the door. "I'll see you ladies later. I have things to do."

"Properly employed," said Mayor Wolfe with authority, "pressure is a useful and effective technique. Not, of course, that I can be officially involved."

"It could work."

"Darn it," snapped Hazel, "will you both

stop talking in riddles?"

Giggling, her face rosy now, her eyes sparkling, Laura didn't answer. She just opened the door and went charging out into the August heat. She didn't stop giggling until she'd reached the hotel. There she went to work.

The first item of business was a telephone call to New York. She got Manny Cohen after two minutes of arguing with his secretary, and she was so steamed up by then she barged right in.

"Mr. Cohen, is it possible for me to speak to Mr. Albright?"

"He's out of town, Miss Staley. I thought my girl had told you that."

"Do you function as his ear, Mr. Cohen, when Mr. Albright isn't available?"

"Eyes and ears, tongue and squawk-box. Not as his checkbook, though. What's on your mind?"

"It isn't convenient for us to house and board your troupe any longer, Mr. Cohen."

He made strangling sounds that could have been laughter, because after half a minute he said: "That was a good one. That really knocked me dead."

"I'm glad you're not distressed, Mr. Cohen. Will you issue instructions for all of them to check out by Saturday?"

"Are you serious?"

"Yes, Mr. Cohen."

"But you can't do that! Why, it's un-American."

Laura hung up. UnAmerican? Well, Mr. Albright would just have to learn the hard way!

Her next item of business was to telephone Mr. Bowser of the *Clarion*. She wasted no time on preliminaries with him, either. "Mr. Bowser, do you have a reporter available?"

"You're a good girl, Laura. It was very kind of you to imply this important newspaper employs someone to do my leg-work. I appreciate that. What's on your mind?"

"I wish to take a full page for Thursday, Mr. Bowser. I can't write, you know that. But I have a message for the community, and if you'll just send someone over to jot down my thoughts —"

"You did say a full page?"

"I did say a full page."

"I'll be over in half an hour."

Laura hung up again and utilized the time to get her thoughts into order. She was interrupted by Mrs. Brigham, who had a problem in bookkeeping she couldn't figure out. Laura figured it out by telling her to forget the problem and to get Pru Drake to the hotel Johnny-quick.

"But this is important, Laura. That twenty-five cents will haunt me. I'll have to list it every month until —"

"This is important, too, Mrs. Brigham. Is this, or is this not, a community that loves fair play?"

"You have been off your feed lately, haven't you?"

Mr. Bowser knocked, came in. Laura waved Mrs. Brigham from the office and motioned Mr. Bowser to a seat. When he was ready she said: "This is in the nature of a protest, Mr. Bowser. It names names, and so you should be careful to print that the views the protest expresses are not your own. I want a great big headline that asks: 'IS THIS FAIR PLAY?' Then I want a picture of Pru Drake under it — posed as that Jewish refugee she played. People loved her in that play. Can do?"

His expression became serious. "Perhaps you'd better tell me the story first."

Laura told him the story, but that was as far as she could get.

Now Mrs. Brigham knocked back and opened the door and came in. "Have you time, Miss Staley, for Mr. Albright? It seems that Mr. Albright has returned to Saunder's Bluff."

Laura swallowed.

"He says it's quite important, Miss Staley."

Mr. Bowser promptly rose, and in the act of so doing betrayed to Laura that her interest in Ken Albright had been noticed by other than her family and close friends.

Blushing, she snapped: "Please sit down, Mr. Bowser. And show Mr. Albright in, Mrs. Brigham, will you, please?"

She borrowed a trick from her father's bag of tricks. She made a tent of her fingers and hands, and was peering down over it at her desk when the big fellow with the shock of golden hair came striding in. She didn't glance up at once. Almost abstractedly she said: "Do sit down, Mr. Albright. I'll be with you in a moment. Now, then, Mr. Bowser, I want it emphatically stated that due to Miss Julie Trotter's rudeness, her unforgivable rudeness, in fact, Miss Drake's nerves were drawn taut and she exploded. This is very important. And don't worry about lawsuits because there were witnesses to the whole thing and —"

Laughter, rich, warm, bouncing laughter, interrupted her. Now she had to look at that handsome face, at those clear blue, sparkling eyes.

"It isn't amusing," she said touchily. "It isn't at all amusing."

"I wasn't laughing at the words, Laura. You were just so girlishly cute in your studied solemnity that I was delighted. Do forgive me, please. And please continue, of course."

She was puzzled. "You want me to continue?"

"Why not? Laura, I served in the Korean War. One of the things we all fought for was the right people have to live, to think. You're entitled to have your views, and to express them."

"You aren't ashamed?"

"Of course I am."

She grew fond of him then, very fond of him. And she began to hope. "Well, then?"

"Business has to be business, Laura."

"And a human being is a human being."

Mr. Bowser got up and made a queer gesture that could have meant anything. "Well, listen," he said. "I'm very busy at the office right now, Laura. So suppose you and Mr. Albright here thresh the thing out. You're too late for this week's edition anyway. Naturally, if you still want to print the protest, I'll be happy to write it and print it for you. All right?"

Laura nodded, but kept her gray eyes looking at Ken Albright. When the door closed she got up and went around to the front of the desk and settled back against its edge. She made a cool, lovely appearance in the simple white pique dress. Her hair, nicely brushed and glossy, seemed to be an intense blue-black in contrast with her face, which was quite pale. Ken, studying her, shrugged. "Nice to see you again, Laura. I missed you."

"I missed you."

He stood up and came toward her but didn't quite touch her. "I never lie, Laura. Do you know that?"

"Ken, that girl's been hurt. What about her?"

"What about all the people in the Broadway show who would suffer heavy loss if Julie were to leave the play?"

"But she couldn't, could she? What about her contract?"

"If she were ill — and that can always be arranged."

"Then you can do nothing?"

"Laura, how long does it take for a woman to forget she once thought she loved someone else?"

She stared.

"Laura —"

"You have to do something, Ken. You do!"

"But —"

"Or I will, Ken. I'm sorry, but I mean that."

He frowned. "Doesn't it mean anything to you that I'm back?"

Laura sighed. That was the trouble, she thought: it did.

CHAPTER 15

And having him back in Saunder's Bluff, not seeing him, not respecting him, really, was worst of all. She deliberately avoided going to the hotel when she knew that he was there. Nor did she answer the telephone when he called. Using the telephone herself, she gave her decision about the troupe to Mr. Williston, and when that had been done she spent as much time as she could at the cottage over near Corkscrew Creek. This vexed her father. "Now listen," he said, "I'm just human enough to want my daughter around the place. Furthermore, you're behaving very badly. I agree you're correct when you state Miss Drake was treated unfairly. But that's no reason for you to shirk your responsibility, or to deprive the hotel of income."

"Do I manage the hotel, Dad, or do you?"

"I believe I retain my ownership of same."

"You all but demanded that I come into the business. I did. Our income over the summer has been higher than almost any summer you can name."

"Nevertheless —"

"And please don't tell me, Dad, that I happened to take over at a lucky time. I played a part in bringing them here. I don't say that the lower rate I gave them brought them here, but it was a big factor when Mr. Albright decided to make the plunge."

"Nevertheless —"

"Anyway, we don't need that kind of money. What about the principle of the thing?"

"Will you listen to me?"

He looked so furious she decided that she better had.

"The fact is," he said, "that you aren't as shrewd as you seem to believe. That's understandable. You haven't any experience to speak of. You're making a serious mistake."

"Name it."

"Mr. Albright's position is reasonable and sound. As the employer of many people, he has a duty to many people. An employer has responsibility, you see. Well, then, in a situation of this kind he must automatically work for the good of the majority. The simple fact is, Laura, that the pain, the disappointment, even the hunger of one person isn't nearly as difficult a burden for your conscience as the pain, the disappointment and the hunger of many persons."

"But —"

"Nor can you blame Albright for a situation not of his making. You must blame the person who caused the situation. In this case Miss Julie Trotter."

"And myself?"

"Yourself?"

"Dad, why do you suppose all this troubles me so? It all happened because of me. Miss Trotter was worried, annoyed. Then she went to the theater. She was trying to show Ken how important she was to him, how kind she could be. She volunteered to play the third act, and that was a big thing to do, her name, her reputation considered. And there, stifling resentment and anger as best she could, she ran into Pru Drake, who'd been in a terrible state of nerves all day. Pru, in a state of nerves, and an apprentice, blew up, and precipitated Miss Trotter's explosion. You see?"

His face grew thoughtful. He pulled his gray brows together in the old way, and swung around in the swivel-chair behind the desk of his paneled study. He gazed out the window at the rear yard. Its fresh green, the roses, the other flowers were inviting. Still, there she was, so young, so troubled, and she was the child of that woman in the painting, and she was his child, too. Gruffly he asked: "Do you love Albright?"

"I'm fond of him, very fond. Is that the same thing?"

"I wouldn't know."

"I don't think so. And I don't think I'm the sort of girl who sails easily from one great love to the next. At least I hope I'm not that sort of girl."

"I fell in love with your mother in ten seconds. I went to your grandfather's house in Beacon Hill one day and caught a glimpse of your mother in the aviary. I fell in love right then."

Laura nodded, touched because he'd never told her that story until then.

"We were happy, too, despite the suddenness of it, despite your grandfather's stuffy, conservative insistence we were being impulsive. Yes, we were impulsive. Actually, most people are. But there can be good sense behind impulse, don't you ever think otherwise."

"I haven't any impulse to marry Ken Albright, Dad."

"I see."

"I'm just not that way. Listen, Dad, rightly or wrongly, I would have married Brad last spring had he wanted me to. I see now that I would have been sorry. I'm using hindsight. Still —"

"About the problem. Why did you drop the only intelligent idea you had?"

Laura was puzzled.

"What was that?"

"Or better still why don't you go to New York and have a frank chat with Julie Trotter?"

"Why, she wouldn't see me!"

He was exasperated, and showed it. He gave the desk a smart slap. "You had a good idea. If Pru Drake was vulnerable because she was an apprentice, without strength, without name, then surely Miss Julie Trotter is vulnerable because she has strength and she has name. Can she risk public obloquy? She cannot."

"Dad!"

"Or better still, get on that telephone and invite her here. Shall I do it for you?"

"But don't you understand —"

He did it for her. There was no nonsense. He didn't permit Miss Trotter's maid to convince him Miss Trotter couldn't possibly come to the telephone. "You will please inform Miss Trotter," he said icily, "that unless she comes to the telephone at once I shall hand this exposure of her character to all the important news services."

Julie Trotter did come to the telephone.

The next afternoon, looking furious, she did come to Saunder's Bluff. Laura, checking the contents of the cottage, heard an automobile horn beep, and when she went outdoors there stood the actress, beautifully dressed, reaching over the fence for the gate latch. When the actress saw her Julie went rigid.

"Do you understand, Miss Staley, that this is tantamount to blackmail?"

"Won't you come in, Miss Trotter? I haven't quite finished tidying up the cottage, but if you wish to have a shower, make a change . . ."

"I do not."

"As you wish, Miss Trotter." Laura smiled as the actress stepped into the yard. She grew aware of an odd thing, that this time, despite the actress' beauty and reputation and aura of glamour, she wasn't awed or impressed a tittle's worth. Now, to her, Julie Trotter was simply another woman, a very lovely woman, but just another human being for all that.

"I was hoping," she said politely, "that you'd be able to stay for a few days. You did say you'd come in August, and here it is just about the end of August."

"The entire concept of the theater was wrong from the beginning. Apprentices learn from example. But Ken refused to believe that in his disgusting greed for large profits. Well, he lost money here, as I told him he would, and his apprentices have learned little, if anything. No. I couldn't possibly associate my name with a project as poorly conceived and operated as that."

"It's too bad," Laura said, and she honestly believed it. "There are so few teachers, there are so few real stars."

Now Julie Trotter did sit down, a crisp, smart figure in her pale gray linen suit. Her black eyes wandered about inquisitively. "I don't hear the frogs," she said.

Laura laughed. "A great many tourists complain because they do hear the frogs." She sat down on the grass and gazed up at Julie Trotter. "You know," she said, "you're quite a woman, Miss Trotter. Do you know what the tragedy is? Your greatest admirer in the troupe wasn't ever Helene Otis, but Pru Drake. I just watched you sit down, and it was like watching Pru Drake sit down. You said 'I don't hear the frogs,' and intonation for intonation, it was Pru Drake speaking. It's almost weird. She must have spent hours watching you, studying you, trying to learn your technique."

"I have no technique. I am simply myself."

"When Pru appeared in that play about the Jewish refugee woman, Miss Trotter, I was sitting beside a critic for one of the New York papers. He said, and I quote: 'There's the finest tribute any actress can be paid — the sincere admiration of an apprentice, the all-out effort of an apprentice to use another actress' technique.' "

Julie Trotter's expression of utter boredom disappeared. She was really very pleased. "He said that?"

"He went on to say, Miss Trotter, that of course Pru Drake could never be you. But he did state that as Pru matured and developed her own personality and technique, there'd be a great star to thank Julie Trotter for."

"Really!"

Now Laura Staley rose. She stood there with her head pushed forward, her young, lovely body stiff with pent-up emotion.

"You're not angry with her, Miss Trotter. How could you be, a great actress, a world-famous star who knows what it is to be all pins and needles and jumping nerves during a performance? You know that in the same set of circumstances you'd have exploded as Pru Drake did and said a great many things you didn't mean."

"Nevertheless —"

"In fact, Miss Trotter, you did explode because you were all pins and needles and jumping nerves."

"You are insufferably and impertinently rude."

"All right! Blame me! Fight me! You'll

probably lick me, too, if that's any encouragement, because I don't have your beauty and glamour and never shall. But in the name of fair play, try to be the person you really are."

"Has Ken proposed to you?"

Laura gasped.

"He told me he would," Julie Trotter said tautly. "I didn't know what to think."

"No, he hasn't."

Julie Trotter grimaced. "I dislike messes. It isn't theater. In the theater there's a nice order, and people behave logically and properly. Yes, I dislike messes."

Laura stood waiting, hoping.

Julie Trotter lifted her voice somewhat, and now into her voice came a lovely, bell-like music that would have carried to a gallery if there'd been a gallery. "But of course, Laura Staley, I cannot permit myself to be bullied or threatened into anything. If one is a star, one has the pride of a star. If one has position, one owes much to that position. If one is a —"

"— human being of dignity," Laura finished, "then one owes it to his dignity to hold firm." She laughed, while Julie Trotter blushed. "They were going to do that play here," she told the actress. "I've heard Pru Drake rehearse that speech over and over again."

"You're utterly impossible!"

"I don't mean to be, Miss Trotter. Believe me, if we can get Pru Drake's career straightened out I won't ever trouble you again."

"But if I don't agree to do as you wish, you'll hand that ridiculous story to the press? You'll vengefully seek to destroy all that I've worked to create?"

Laura tried to say that she would. It was what she wanted to say, because she had the strong conviction that the threat was a club that would win the day for Pru. Yet she couldn't say it! It suddenly occurred to her that she couldn't say it because she could never bring herself to hand that story to Mr. Bowser, let alone the great news services of the country. When you destroyed you just destroyed. You never created anything, and what was ever the good of destruction?

"Well? Speak up, please!"

Laura sat down again, her knees wobbly. "No," she muttered, baffled, annoyed with herself, "I wouldn't do that."

"But your father said —"

"I know. But I've seen you in many plays, and they were beautiful plays, and you're beautiful, too, and — darn it, I'd like to slap your face!"

Incredibly, Julie Trotter laughed. Nor was it a stage laugh; it was a good, old-fashioned, human laugh that came all the way up from her stomach to hang in the air almost a minute.

Flushing, Laura rose. She felt confused, upset, angry with herself, ashamed of herself. Fine! See how she'd flubbed it!

"Laura?"

"Well?"

"Do you have any notion why I came here? Ken and I are finished. My contract carries to next June, and it won't be renewed. I've already tentatively accepted an offer from another producer. I may go into motion-pictures, television, I don't quite know. So you see that club of yours wasn't a club at all."

Laura turned, her eyes wide, her lips parted.

"However, it doesn't matter. I've been a very foolish woman, Laura. I've always assumed that because I wanted something another person would want it, too. But Ken didn't. He never did, he never will, and the rest doesn't matter."

"I —"

"Well, why not? Exit gracefully, Frank Jones always says, and perhaps it pleases me to do so. Shall I please you, dear Laura, dear country girl, dear girl of so many illusions? Shall I be the great and beautiful star who will live always in your mind?"

"Be still!" Laura snapped. "If you spoil it I will slap your face!"

Their eyes locked. Now the sound of Corkscrew Creek behind the house grew louder and louder and louder. Laura heard the wind in the birches and beeches and willows — then the distant, melancholy croak of a frog.

"What would I spoil?" Julie Trotter asked.

"What you are. An actress is the beauty she creates, isn't she? A part of her must be. All any actress can do is reflect something she is within."

"You are a child, aren't you?"

Laura pitied her. And if all actresses were as blind to their own beauty as Julie Trotter was, then she pitied all the actresses who'd ever lived.

"Well," she asked, "will you do it?"

"Why not? Perhaps it pleases my vanity to have somewhere on this globe a slavish admirer and imitator such as Pru. By the way, what was the name of that New York critic who said those lovely things about me?"

Laura told her.

Julie Trotter smiled. "What a nice surprise! I must give him lunch some day soon."

Her exit was graceful after all.

Queerly, the lovely countryside seemed dull, very dull, after Julie Trotter was gone.

Swallowing hard, Laura went back into the cottage. She asked Pru Drake: "Well, did you hear?"

Pru Drake sighed. "Her laughter was crude, didn't you think? Personally, I'd have kept it a bit more restrained. . . ."

CHAPTER 16

The sentimental man was deeply pleased. "I love you, too," he said, "and if you ever need a dime just come ask me." He paused, his wrinkled, middle-aged face flushed with emotion. Then he continued softly, huskily: "You understand, don't you, that Pru the human has nothing to do with Pru the actress? I dislike Pru the human as much as anyone does. But she can give such pleasure as an actress. Don't laugh. Give me three years with her, and a girl such as you will be terribly disappointed that all she ever saw of Pru, real close up, was her pumps getting into a cab. It happens. It will happen this time, because I'm Frank Jones and I know talent when I see it."

Laura liked him then. She thought that of all the Albright troupe that had come to Saunder's Bluff for the summer, this stocky, middle-aged man was the most human. What he felt for his profession, his art, was felt deeply. But what he felt for human beings was felt deeply, too. She was very glad she had met Frank Jones. She would remember all through her life, she decided, that it was important to help people regardless of what your personal opinions of them were. Perhaps she would be a better person all her life because one summer in Vermont she'd made the acquaintance of Frank Jones.

"Will you be back next year?" she asked.

"Who knows? The Players will be, sure. This was a good summer. We broke even, the boss tells me, and our last two weeks here will give us a little profit. But Frank Jones, personally? Who knows? I could go to Hollywood, you know. They need geniuses out there, now that television is murdering them."

"Well, if you do come out here next summer, Frank, I think I'll establish you in the cottage. It's very lovely there. It may inspire you, as it did me."

"I wish," he said "that I could have seen the performance. When Julie came here she was practically purring. She said something that tells me you were as good an actress in that scene as she ever was. She said that one of these days she's going to mail you a nice gift because you're one of the sweetest admirers she's ever had. Did you enlarge those lines I gave you to recite?"

Laura was about to tell him that at the last

minute she'd thrown all his carefully dreamed up lines to the winds, that when she'd begun to take a grip on her nerves she'd found it possible to speak naturally and warmly from her heart. But why spoil Frank's little hour of "triumph"? Why dwell on any of it? It was all over. Pru was a member of the Albright Players again, Pru would repeat her smash performance in that play involving the Jewish refugee woman. People would see Pru and hear her and be thrilled. They might even remember, watching and listening to Pru in that death scene, that not too many years ago the Germany now being hailed as a stout and true friend of Democracy was the Germany that had butchered millions of helpless human beings and had plunged the world into a ghastly war that had destroyed many millions more. Or was that too much to hope for?

She got up from the bench before the barn-theater. It was coming on toward evening. Far across the farmland the hills were already purple, and there was Brad driving his tractor in for the day, and there were the birds flying to wherever it was that they spent the night.

"Frank?"

"Yes?"

"Does Pru spend much time with Brad, now that she's an actress again?"

He turned and looked at the fellow on the

tractor. "It would be silly. If you want something with all your heart and soul, you can't forget that, you can't turn your back on it. No, she doesn't see him any more. He doesn't see you any more. It's sensible, that. She wants the theater; he wants his wealth, his security. But don't waste time feeling sorry for him or sorry for Pru. In time it all works out for the best."

Yet she did feel sorry, for Brad at least, as she watched him drive the tractor into his yard. He was covered with dust and dirt. He was very thin and very nervous. He was getting on, and he'd be wealthy some day, no doubt of it. But how alone and lonely he looked there on his farm, against the graying Vermont sky.

Should she go over to him, say a few friendly words? Well, why not? She was a Saunder's Bluff girl; he was a Saunder's Bluff fellow. What was behind them was behind them. It hadn't been intended, obviously, and since that was so, why should either she or Brad feel bitter?

She turned to Frank, held out her hand. "Well, I'll see you, Frank. You'll be gone when I return from Boston, but perhaps I'll go to New York this winter to see Julie in that play. If so, may I take you to dinner?"

"Why not? Money's made to be spent, and

you have money."

"It's a date!"

"Also," he said tenderly, "you're a decent girl with a heart. I'm always a sucker for girls like you. A real thrill. I'll even wear a necktie."

Quickly, before she could change her mind, Laura hurried over to the old frame house which she'd once dreamed of occupying in the role of Mrs. Brad Holbrook. She swung around the corner of the house and stood waiting near the old well for Brad to come in from the tractor shed. His nervous start and his frown, when he did so, made her wonder if she'd been intelligent after all.

"Hello," she said simply. "I'm making a kind of tour, saying goodbye to this one, to that."

"Goodbye?"

She tossed her lovely black head. "Oh, it's Boston again for a while. You know my Gramps. He says autumn isn't in the wind until I'm there to bully him into wearing his winter underwear. I'll be gone a month or so."

He nodded, smiled faintly. "Leaving before the Players, huh? You should stick around at least to see Pru in that play."

"Oh, I saw her rehearse that part. About Pru, Brad, you mustn't think that I —"

"I know, I know. But you know something, Laura? I guess I'm like those hills, this farm. I don't change much. I know a lot of people thought that because I was with her so much I was trying to get over you. That's bunk. She was a farm kid. I felt sorry for her. That was all it ever was."

"Fine!"

"And you? Well, Laura, the way I've figured it all out is this. I love you, but I guess not the way I always thought. I mean, that was always the trouble. We always quarreled and carried on because we wasn't working toward the same thing, not really. I guess I always wanted a little bit more than I had, and I guess in the pinch that little bit more than I had was more important to get than you were. It's funny. I feel good now, real good. I guess I'll hate leaving this place, because here's where I figured it all out and got to know myself. Still, with all that money —"

"Brad, you're selling out?"

His brown eyes gleamed. "Look, I can be a big success. This proves it. You think I didn't hope, when I leased that barn to him, that maybe one of these days he'd want the rest, too? Sure I did. It just had to be! A fellow doing good business will naturally want the place his business stands on."

"You've sold this place to Ken Albright?"

"After the crops are in, after I've had a chance to get my things taken away."

"Brad, what a shame. Why, it won't seem like Saunder's Bluff without a single Holbrook living here. Brad, how could you? Why, your folks cleared this land!"

"There's always land. There isn't always thirty-five thousand in cash."

"Just the same —"

"Ah, let's not scrap. It's part of what I was saying before, Laura. To me the cash is important."

"I see."

"You marrying Albright?"

"Brad, don't be silly!"

Strangely disturbed, she couldn't stand there talking to him any longer. She felt shocked deep to her core. How dreadful to sell your home, your farm, for mere cash! If you had to do so, that was one thing. But to do so simply because it seemed good business!

"Well, keep in touch with me, Brad. If you ever need or want anything, just write me, will you? Brad, I know I said and did some rather hot-tempered things here one day, but I am very fond of you."

"Sure."

She turned quickly and made her way back through the September cool to her Ford.

She found Ken Albright in it, waiting. It

was the fifth evening in a row that she'd found him there, amiably awaiting a free ride back to the Staley Hotel. He should be charged a dollar each time, she thought, only if she did do that and the sum was dutifully entered on the hotel's books by Mrs. Brigham, someone could claim she was operating a commercial vehicle without a proper license. The thought made her chuckle.

"Grand evening coming on, isn't it?" he asked, encouraged. "I love the way twilight comes here. Very slowly and gently at first, and all the world seems to shrink. Then a quick, quick rush of dark, and it's night."

She started the car and turned on her dim lights and guided the car to the highway. "I just love everything here," she told him. "But I'm prejudiced. I'm a Saunder, or part of me is. My great-greats established the first farm in this area. Gradually, others came. And one day, so the legend goes, along came a war party of Indians, too. Jacob Saunder, the man they named this town for, went charging out with his rifle. Those Indians were surrounded, he said, and if they didn't throw down their arms he'd give the signal to send them all to the Happy Hunting Grounds. They threw down their arms, and you've guessed it — the Indians weren't surrounded at all. So they call this place Saunder's Bluff, and it's all bred into my very bones, and this is where I'll live always, and this is where my children will be born and raised."

She was sitting quite relaxed behind the steering-wheel. Her head was gracefully poised, there was a soft smile on her lips, there was good rich color in her cheeks. Ken Albright noticed all these things, and nodded.

"I understand," he said.

"Brad tells me you've bought his farm."

"It was for sale, and I love it."

"It's good land. I don't think Brad has ever gotten from it the crops he should, but if it's carefully reworked and fertilized, it ought to yield a good return on your investment."

"Laura?"

In an unnatural, thin voice she said: "I'm going to Boston, Ken. Summer's almost gone, and I'm a bit tired, and my Gramps is lonely for some bullying."

"Aren't you ashamed to bully anyone?"

"Not Gramps. My Grammy bullied him for years, and he loved it. Gramps says I remind him of my Grammy. That's interesting, because my Dad says I remind him of my mother."

"No doubt," he teased, "it's your cutting little tongue."

Laura drove on. The twilight was thickening now, and here and there across fields and farmlands she saw lights shining cheerily in solitary houses. It was very nice to be driving across such land at such a time with Ken Albright big and handsome beside her. A part of her wished the hour could be stretched into a kind of never-changing forever.

"I have a date with Frank for dinner this winter in New York."

"I'm jealous."

She drew a quick breath.

He noticed.

"I retract that, Laura. I have no right to feel jealous. There's so much time in New England that a year's just a day, and I should remember that. We've barely met, isn't that so?"

"Barely."

"And you're never carried away by impulse?"

"I prefer not to be. I like to know what I'm doing, and why I'm doing it."

"But how much time is there, Laura?"

She wouldn't help him, she thought, because it was too soon, whether he laughed at her or held that laughter in.

He slid closer.

But that was all right, she thought, because there were the lights of the town, and in a pinch she could always scream for help.

"I won't hurry you," Ken Albright said.

"But I will say something to demonstrate I'm a sturdy fellow of character and that my intentions are quite honorable. I will say, Laura, that I love you. I love you very much. I concede I haven't given the matter much thought, and that perhaps the whole thing is impulsive. But I'm from the West, myself, and it's in my nature to make snap decisions. So actually I'm being true to my heritage when I say, without qualification, reservation or even inebriation, I love you."

She had to laugh.

Thus encouraged, he took one of her hands from the steering wheel and raised it to his lips.

Laura felt warm, quivery.

She drove by the hotel, despite the shouts of the Albright Players loitering before its entrance door.

"There," said Ken Albright. "Now perhaps you had better let me out. Incidentally, I haven't yet thanked you for the way you handled that problem for me. It was decent of you, Laura, to accomplish it all without using that club. Thank you."

She nodded and drove on, turned into Franklin D. Roosevelt Avenue.

"Well, it'll be grand to see Pru in that play tonight, Laura, won't it?"

"I'm not going."

"Incidentally, where are we going?"

She turned right into James Monroe Street. This, she remembered, was where it had all begun one day back in early May when she'd been chatting with Mayor Wolfe, and the big fellow with the shock of golden hair had gone by to stop under a maple tree and fill and light his pipe. How strange, she thought. Now she was in business with her father, now the Brad problem was no longer a problem, now she knew what she really wanted and why she wanted it. Such a queer summer of work and tension, of making new friends, of learning the worth of all her old friends. And now autumn was coming and the summer was almost gone and Brad was selling out and the new owner of the Holbrook farm was there beside her.

"Ken?"

"Yes, Laura?"

"When I first saw you on this street you very carefully looked from house to house. And Mayor Wolfe was with me and asked what on earth you were seeing. Well, what were you seeing?"

"Look straight ahead, Laura."

"Uh-huh."

"Now what do you see from the corners of your eyes?"

"More houses."

"But if someone were standing in one of

those yards, wouldn't you see that someone?"

"Well, I — Ken Albright!"

"Sure," he chuckled. "I was seeing you, Laura."

She turned into her father's drive and parked the car near the front porch. She got out and led him up the stoop to the porch. "Since you're here," she said casually, "you may as well have dinner with us."

But he'd waited long enough, had Ken Albright. He turned her about, very gently, but firmly. "Laura, I know it's really too soon. Understand that I know that. But would you be able to say if I do stand a chance?"

She blushed, but nodded.

"Thank you, Laura."

"You're welcome, Ken."

"Laura, could I —"

"Would you be here, Ken, if you couldn't?"

It took a moment for that to penetrate. Then his arms went about her. "Laura, darling."

"I just need a vacation, Ken, a chance to think. Then if you're still so impulsive —"

But that was as far as she could get. And in his arms, with his lips on hers, Laura Staley thought it really didn't matter. Kisses spoke, too. He was her man! And if she wasn't his girl this was definitely a scandal!

Was it a scandal?

She drew back and looked up into those burning blue eyes.

No, she thought, it wasn't a scandal. In time it would be the dream, the big dream. It would be the only reality that would ever matter.

"Ken," she said, "Ken, darling, let's eat. There'll be time for that later on. . . ."

She turned happily and opened the big front door.

LP MAR
Marsh, Rebecca
Summer in Vermont